Tales From Under the Nook

A Sequel to Tales From Under the Crevice
By Zephyr Goza

www.crevicetales.com

The green people are back!

Zephyr Goza

The following work is a work of total, utter, and absolute…well, I wouldn't say fiction…maybe a couple of stretches of the truth…but not exactly fiction. Oh, hey, who the ding hey am I kidding? Fairies? Dragons? I must have made this up, right? No way it could be true. No way *(I can't tell the truth now because the little people are watching you)* at all. Or is there?

If you are still reading this, you either have issues or you are a librarian, which I suppose are synonymous. In any case, it is an excellent idea to skip the rest of the copyright page and begin reading the rest of the book. Do not, however, skip ahead to the ending. I have worked very hard to transcribe the events that happened to me in the crevice world, and I will probably get upset if you do that. That's just plain cheap.

Hey, I just realized that only I have the power to make you stop reading the copyright page! If I stop writing this, then your only option is to stop reading! Cool! I have complete and total control over you. I could copy and paste the entire text of *Huckleberry Finn* right here and certain people would still read the whole thing! This is fun!

This is the end of the copyright page. The legal stuff is over. Just go to the story, please.

For all the people whose names I am too lazy to write here.

Chapter 1
A Return

"Once upon a time in a faraway land…" is a phrase that is said to be used to begin many fantasy tales. However, in reality, very few tales actually begin with "Once upon a time in a faraway land…". This is one of the few.

However, you should also understand that this is hardly a fantasy tale. If you came looking for a fantasy book, you won't be disappointed here. All the same, this is not a fantasy tale. These events really happened. However, before you can understand the events in this book, you should probably go read a book called *Tales From Under the Crevice*. Go purchase a copy. Of course, if you already have a copy, maybe you should purchase another one. It can't hurt. In fact, you should buy two or three more.

Anyway, this book takes place four days after that book. For those shameless persons who are still reading this even though they have not yet read my other book (shame on you, you shamefully shameless people), this book takes place inside a green '95 Chevy conversion van towing a trailer that, I'm quite happy to report, is brand new and has been customized with our theatre company's logo. The utility trailer is filled to the brim with props, sets, costumes, camping equipment, so on, and so forth. The reason the trailer is filled with such strange stuff is because my family (my mother, my father, and a fourteen-year-old novelist and Halloween fanatic) is a traveling theatre troupe with no permanent home. Really. Don't believe me? Go to www.activated-storytellers.com. The proof is there.

Like I said, this book takes place four days after *Tales From Under the Crevice*. Our lifestyle often causes us to sleep in the van. My sleeping bag is placed between two seats, with my head underneath the seat that folds out flat to become my parents' bed. Their blankets hang down over the edge, sealing my head in pitch black.

Anyway, one night I was lying down to sleep in the nook. I had just adjusted my head on my pillow and was dozing off when I felt something tugging on my hair. I turned my head. Nothing was there. I dismissed it as nothing but my imagination and returned to thinking about an interesting dream I'd had the other night involving little green people, a really bad guy, and a very tall tree. I was just drifting off again when I felt another little tug. I rolled over and something scampered across my face. Startled, I began to sit up…

…And I started to shrink. The floor dropped out from under me. I swirled around in nothingness for a moment. Then I landed with a soft *plop* on my pillow. And then I came to the sudden realization that I hadn't been dreaming about little green people, a really bad guy, and a really tall tree. Maybe it hadn't all been a figment of my imagination. I whispered the name of one of the people from my dream just to be sure. "Serrin?"

"Ha!" said the pair of glowing red eyes now bobbing in front of me. "I'm back!"

"Why?" I said. "What happened? What's the matter?"

"Nothing unusual has happened. We just…haven't seen you in a while." I rather doubted this to be true, since Serrin had a knack for concealing ulterior motives.

"A while? It's only been four days!"

"Days? Zephyr, we haven't seen you in almost four years!" Then it slowly sunk in. Hadn't Serrin said something about this last time? Something about how time moves more quickly in the crevice world?

"All right, all right." I said. "I'll come down for a visit. But I can only stay for a few days." Without another word, he dashed off between the small cardboard boxes stored by my pillow. I followed him. We ran under a black metal bar supporting my parents' bed and around a corner. Then we entered an air conditioning vent in the back of the van, and felt our way along the walls.

And then the wind hit me in the face. I felt the familiar sensation of plunging several stories in pitch black. The crevice world slowly faded into view from the darkness that surrounded us. I was now sliding down the trunk of a giant palm tree a mile high towards a little patch of sand far below. After several minutes, it rushed up to hit me square in the nose. It didn't hurt in the slightest bit. The sand was incredibly soft. I pushed myself up and jumped to my feet. None of these events surprised me a bit. I was actually slightly used to having little green people interrupt my sleep. And I had experienced this sudden drop into the crevice world once before. But, of course, you would know that if you had read my other book like you were supposed to.

Serrin leaped up and jumped into the water instantly. There I got my first good look at Serrin in four days (years, I suppose). He really had changed. He still wore his purple hair in a part down the middle, hanging down to his cheeks on either side. His ears were sharper, and he was a few inches taller.

"What happened to your face, mate?" he inquired. I peered into the water.

"That would be the footprints of a certain Glunch who scampered all over my face."

"Oops," he grinned sheepishly. "Sorry."

I slipped into the water and washed off my face. I felt a funny, damp sensation as I did this. Like everything else in the crevice world, the water here had strange properties. Namely, it wasn't wet. Well, parts of it were. If the water was blue, it was wet. If it was green, however, it remained dry. I had just washed my face with water that wasn't wet. The little patch of sand was surrounded by a mixed river of green and blue that encompassed it. On both sides were lush, tropical jungles. These jungles were separated by the river that split around the patch of sand. I assumed that the river led out to sea.

"Come on, then." said Serrin. We splashed our way to the opposite shore. He led me through the thick jungle until we came to a bamboo ladder.

"Hey, what's this?" I asked. "This wasn't here before."

"The village transportation system," Serrin said casually.

"You guys added a transportation system?"

"One of us did," he said, climbing the ladder. I followed him up. We stood on a wooden platform about thirty-five feet high. A ten foot high wooden pole sat in the middle of the platform. Attached to the pole was a rope that led into the jungle. A wooden box was attached to the rope by means of another rope. A metal hook attached the box to the platform.

"Here we are," said Serrin, climbing into the box. "Just room enough for two." I squeezed in beside him.

"So…how does this work?" My question was answered a little too quickly when he flipped the metal hook. We slid down the rope all too fast, the bottom of the box clipping trees. Then we were crashing through a tangled mess of limbs and leaves. We erupted out of the greenery just under the tree line and sped towards the ground just as we reached the village outskirts. Then we came to a screeching halt. Unfortunately, I was ill prepared for this. I went flying through the air and landed several feet away, whereupon I noticed two things.

The first was that I had managed to land directly in the midst of a young group of girls who appeared to be having some sort of social gathering involving tea. They were staring at me rather awkwardly. One of them had started to take a bite of a scone, but was now rapidly scooting back in fear. The rest followed her example.

The next was that the village had been completely rebuilt. The last time I had visited, it was in charred, smoldering ruins because of an intentionally set fire. This time, though, it was rebuilt better than before. The bamboo buildings were clean and fresh, each with an architectural elegance its predecessor had not achieved.

"Wow," I stammered, standing up. "Who rebuilt this?"

"I did," replied the one girl who had not instantly shied away. She was casually leaning against a tree, staring up at me. She was about my own age, with deep, calculating purple eyes and blue hair pulled back into a ponytail accompanied by heavy bangs and two long locks of hair that hung down over her temples. A pair of goggles was pulled up over her head. She wore loose, baggy pants and a grimy white shirt, along with fingerless gloves on her hands. "I also designed the transportation system," she continued. "Although Serrin still hasn't learned to properly operate the brakes yet." She shot a withering glance in his direction. Wincing, he came forward.

"Zephyr, this is Kimara, our transportation specialist and engineer," he said before quickly retreating.

"Engineer, huh? I don't think we've met," I said.

"We haven't," Kimara replied. "But I have seen you before. The last time you were here."

"Ah," I said. "Well, yes, um, nice to meet you." Here I extended my hand to shake. The rest of the girls leaned closer, staring in excitement as to what would happen next. When she shook my hand, they all relaxed visibly.

In a couple of hours' time I was in the pub drinking slurk with some of my old buddies. You have probably not heard of slurk. This means you have never been to the crevice world, and if you have, you weren't paying attention. Slurk is a thick, delicious drink, sort of like eggnog. Serrin likes slurk. I like slurk. It would appear that Kimara does not like slurk. She stared at Serrin and I as if we were drinking worms. Instead of slurk, she drank some sort of green tea and sat on the indoor balcony of the pub (which she must have helped build, since it had been a single story the last time I had been there). Serrin and I were talking rather animatedly about what had happened in the time we'd been apart, although we exaggerated several things for the benefit of the group of girls, who had now decided that I was okay after all and had taken to crowding around us.

I was taking a particularly large gulp of slurk when somebody popped up beside me—somebody very familiar. "Long time, no see, eh?" said the slender form that was Bednik.

"Bednik!" I cried. "How have you been?"

"Not so good after Ragnark died, but I'm doing fine now. Where have you been?"

"Up in my world, where I've been attending to my...*other* life." I said, allowing a moment of silence for Ragnark. Ragnark had been a great friend of ours who had died in battle with a very evil person named Ranook.

Anyway, we sat around drinking slurk with our friend Morn (who lived with different little green people called Galians in the tall red palm tree) into the wee hours of the morning, when we finally shuffled off into the darkness, each going his own way. I found a nice, soft, mossy spot under some ferns and fell asleep. Even though so much had changed, it was great to make a return.

Chapter 2
Kimara

The first thing I was aware of were eyes. Two eyes were floating directly above mine. And then I realized that the eyes belonged to a face. A green female face.

I jumped backwards, tripped over a stone, and fell into the soft soil. I panicked for a moment, trying to figure out why I had just managed to wake up in the middle of a forest with a green-skinned girl I didn't know kneeling over me. Then my memory came flooding back. I had forgotten that I was in the crevice world.

"There you are," Kimara giggled. "I was looking all over for you. Serrin's got something he wants you to see." she grabbed me by the hand and dragged me off through the woods.

"Wait!" I cried as we ran by a stream. "I'm not even awake yet!" I suppose it was when she grabbed my head that I realized she had a unique way of solving problems. Or maybe it was as she pushed it down. Or maybe it was as my face splashed into the stream. In any case, I definitely knew it by the time I jumped up coughing and sputtering. "What was that for?" I yelled.

"Well, you're awake now, aren't you?" she said innocently. Unable to dispute the fact, I continued on, coughing and sputtering.

We kept going until we reached a small tent, which I recognized as the one Serrin stayed in. He was standing outside waiting for us. "There you are, Zephyr!" he said. "I think this may interest you." he pulled out a musty old volume and laid it open on a rock near the tent.

"What's this?" I asked.

"It's a journal," he said.

"Whose?"

"Panok's." I stared at it in silence. Panok was the founder of Serrin's village, which was named, appropriately enough, Panok. But you should know that already because you should have read my other—oh, all right, I'll stop. "The point is, Zephyr, with this we can make all kinds new discoveries about this world! Things we never knew before! Perhaps we can even create a detailed history!"

"So…that's what you brought me down here for, then?"

"I…um…"

"Basically, yes." said Kimara matter-of-factly. "He's been wanting to do this with your help for months." Serrin winced. I sighed. Sure enough, there was the ulterior motive.

"When and how do we start?" I said. Serrin relaxed visibly.

"Well," Kimara coughed. "I have been working on something…" we both winced this time. After my little encounter with her transportation system, I was not exceptionally eager to have any more experiences with Kimara's technology.

But within seconds we were being dragged of to an undisclosed location, Kimara chattering excitedly. I could have sworn I saw a footprint on the ground somewhere that did not belong to one of us. I wanted to stop and inspect it, but Kimara grabbed me by the arm and kept dragging me onwards. We passed through the village until we came to a wooden building in a small clearing away from the village.

Here she stopped for a moment to open the door to the shed. It was quite dark inside. "Where are we?" I asked cautiously.

"Inside my workshop." she responded.

"I didn't know she *had* a workshop!" Serrin whispered. Then the doors creaked shut behind us. We sat there in the dark for a moment as we heard some liquid being funneled through pipes all around us. Then a single match lit by Kimara's face and ventured into a lamp, where it roared into a fire. Kimara shut the door on the lantern as the flame spread rapidly to other lanterns through a complicated network of pipes and tubes. The shed instantly lit up—and with the light came heat.

And with the heat came a view of the shed. Besides the maze of pipes and lanterns, there were various tools and devices hanging up along the walls; a pile of scrap wood was stacked up in one corner; a pile of stones in another; ropes and aprons sat on a table; a shelf of jars and boxes stamped *Imported From Shanar* sat on one wall; on another shelf could be found various solid and liquid fuels.

But quite easily the most distinguishing item sat in the middle of the shed. It was a large wooden platform. The platform rested upon four stone wheels. These wheels were held together by large metal axles. In the middle of the platform was a seat. The seat was surrounded by various levers and poles. The poles extended up nearly to the roof of the workshop. They had a joint in the middle so they could bend, and each one was equipped with a different tool at the end. One was a pair of shears, another was the head of a shovel, another was a clamp for grabbing things, another a crane, and another still an axe. A pair of metal arms was folded up behind the chair. One ended in a clip for holding things. The other contained a series of magnifying glasses on top of one another. The glasses were held together with a screw so they could fold out. A pair of tubes pointed outwards from the front of the contraption. A box of harpoons sat on either side in front. A large stove sat just behind the seat. The back was piled up high with packs and supplies. The perimeter was secured with a rope fence held up by wooden poles, complete with a gate held with a clip.

"Wow." said Serrin. "Wow…what is this?"

"APLEV." She responded, smiling.

"What?" I said.

"APLEV. All Purpose Land Exploration Vehicle."

I was in shock. I had seen some pretty ingenious stuff in this world—especially for people with such a low level of technology—but this took the cake. "W—what does it do?" I stammered.

"Exactly what the name implies. It's a vehicle for explorers. It is capable of carrying supplies and villagers. It uses the heat of fire to spin the axle, so it can move about as fast as you can walk. In case we can't use fire, there's a backup water pump system. It's made for all types of land terrain and can explore ruins and hostile environments quite well, given room." We just sat and stared in awe. "Well, um…what do you think?"

"It's—it's ingenious! You built this?" I said in shock.

"She would disappear for hours—even days— at a time," said Serrin. "Now I know where to…and why."

"It really is…" I started laughing. "It really is a clever contraption. You designed it?"

"Designed it and built it," she said, blushing with pride.

"Let's find the others and get going," said Serrin.

Chapter 3
Expedition

I watched the stone wheel kick up dust as I walked behind the APLEV. Bednik, Serrin, and Morn walked beside me. We had deposited our packs on the APLEV, but chosen to walk ourselves.

Serrin had been quite eager to leave, so there was barely any time to pack. Serrin had a small band of Glunches called the Guard. Their mission basically had been to search for humans, but since he had found me, they seemed to be only pack mules, or whatever else was convenient. In the village, they became pack mules. Serrin had them going back and forth preparing for our trip. They were now asleep on the back of the APLEV.

"So…where are we going again?" I asked.

"We're looking for the third brother," said Serrin. "Or, more specifically, his village."

"His village?" Morn said skeptically.

"Correct. The villages of Panok and Shanar were named, according to Panok's journal, after two of three brothers. The journal only makes vague references to a third village, but this map…" he pulled out the journal and dumped a folded map from between the pages. "…marks a specific location."

"When did you find this thing?" I asked.

"Last time you were here, when I temporarily dismantled the temple. It took me four years to translate because Panok had a habit of writing in the old language."

"Speaking of that old temple, did you ever get it back together?" Serrin coughed uncomfortably. I took that as a no.

I guess I should not have been surprised when Serrin opted for a more "direct" route through the fields of wheat that occupied the plains. Fortunately, I was no longer in my pajamas, having changed into more adventurous gear (boots, a pair of leather gloves, a loose white shirt, and a baggy pair of gray pants secured with a red cloth in use as a belt) prior to leaving. This meant that the tall stalks of wheat were no problem. However, the fog was rolling in much thicker, making it much more difficult to see. In addition, I could have sworn I felt something biting my ankle. I shook my leg a bit and it went away. A few seconds later, it was back. I kicked hard this time. "OW!" I yelled. A small brown figure came flying through the air.

"Everyone on the APLEV!" Morn yelled, leaping onto the platform. I followed suit. Kimara slowed the vehicle to a stop.

"What was that?" I said, rubbing my ankle.

"Field gnomes," Morn said tensely. The small brown figure clambered up onto the platform with us. It was about two feet tall with brown skin. Its short brown arms ended in stubby little fingers. It wore only a loincloth. The head was round, interrupted by odd lumps and bald save for a tuft of dark hair at the top. The eyes were mismatched. One was large and green, the other was small and purple. The gnome had an under-bite that left its square teeth exposed. The nose was long and crooked.

"What are you doing here?" it squeaked. I had to stop myself from laughing. This thing was supposed to be a threat?

"Just passing through," said Morn, but I noticed that his hand was on the hilt of his sword.

"Passing through?" said the gnome. "No one is welcome here for *any* reason!"

"Well, then, we'll just be on our way," replied Morn. "Just as soon as we…"

"On your way?" laughed the gnome. "I think not." There was a trampling sound all around us as the stalks of wheat shook. "ATTACK!" cried the gnome. "KILL THE…" a boot kicked him off the platform. Kimara casually walked back to her seat and started the vehicle moving again as the little gnome tried to climb back up on the APLEV. Morn sighed.

"Well, I tried to handle that diplomatically." he said. "I usually don't like to bother with the little runts. They always like to make trouble. They seem to think they own the wheat fields. I just like to let them think so and keep going. They can bite, though, so it's important to keep your feet off the ground."

"OW!" I heard a familiar voice scream in the background. "STUPID GNOMES! SHOO! OFF WITH YOU!" A few more of the brown figures flew through the air.

"Now, now, relax—ow—I'm sure they—ow— don't mean any harm."

"No harm? No harm? Oh, it would be fitting to die at the hands of a bunch of weak little brown— ow—whatever they are!"

"Now, now, Bulrog…"

"It's Bulrog and Gorlub!" I yelled.

"I thought it was Gorlub and Bulrog," said Bednik.

"One way or the other, here they come!" I said. Two shapes emerged from the fog; one was tall and thin, the other short and fat. They were half-hopping, half-running, slapping at their feet and kicking field gnomes into the air.

"Gorlub! Bulrog!" I yelled. They looked up.

"Oh, lovely!" yelled Bulrog (the short, fat one with a B embroidered on his sweater). "A group of bilabial fricatives on a giant pile of firewood! Just what we needed!" Bulrog had a bit of a pessimistic disposition, in case you hadn't guessed.

Kimara stopped the APLEV and jumped down, marching over to Bulrog. "What…did you call…my APLEV?" she hissed, bristling.

"Why…it's…it's…Zephyr!" stuttered Gorlub (the tall, thin one with a G embroidered on his sweater). "Zephyr and Serrin and Morn and Bednik!" He blinked, and then broke into a wide grin. "How are you doing? Where have you been? What's going on?"

"Come on up and I'll explain," Morn said, helping him up. Gorlub climbed on, completely ignoring Bulrog's terrified screams. Kimara was now chasing him around the APLEV with a large rock she had found who knows where.

I will draw the curtain of privacy over the rest of this scene for Bulrog's sake. Suffice it to say that he wound up on the APLEV several minutes later with quite a few bruises, where Gorlub explained to him the mission we were on.

We were now drawing closer to the edge of the wheat fields. The sun was sinking rapidly into dusk. "All right," Serrin announced. "We'll set up camp just inside the forest." He grabbed his pack and slung it over his shoulder, ready to disembark. Kimara stopped the APLEV several hundred feet into the forest. Serrin promptly hopped off. I heard a shuffle and a thud in the dark. "Ow." Serrin's voice penetrated the darkness. A match was lit somewhere. An intense flash lit up the night. Serrin was getting up from the ground, shielding his eyes against the bright light. By the time my eyes adjusted, I realized that I was looking at the light from a pair of lanterns up front that served as headlights. Kimara had ingeniously fashioned torches inside them, making the sides out of magnifying glass so as to intensify the light.

"Wow," said Serrin. "Thanks."

"No problem," she said. "But next time, let me turn on the light *before* you fall all over yourself in the dark."

The tents were set up around the APLEV, with a fire in the middle built for cooking. The cooks broke into our food supply and began making the night's meal. Serrin got out Panok's journal and some parchment and began making notes with a quill. Kimara inspected the APLEV carefully, and then wandered off into the woods somewhere.

I sat around the fire with Serrin and Bednik, watching the cooks boil some strange kind of pasta entirely unique to the crevice world. Where else can you find turquoise pasta?

Anyway, I was about to start eating when Kimara came sliding (quite literally) into camp in a very dramatic fashion. "Zephyr!" she said excitedly. "You have to come see this!" I sighed and reluctantly put down my bowl of turquoise pasta.

"Now what?" I sighed.

"Did you find the village of the third brother?" yelped Serrin excitedly. She just shook her head, smiled slightly at Serrin, and dragged me off into the forest. We ran a short way until we came to the edge of a cliff. Well, actually, it was a waterfall. We were standing at the edge of a river that flowed into a waterfall. Steam rose from the blue pool below indicating that besides being wet, it was warm. The surrounding area sort of sloped into a basin, which contained the pool.

"That's it?" I said blankly. "You brought me here just to show me a waterfall and a pool?"

"Well, wouldn't you like to go for a swim?"

"Yeah, sure I would, but that's beside the…oh, wait…no way…" my protest came too late. The next thing I knew, I had fallen ten feet or so, been submerged in warm water, and come to the surface. Kimara helped me out, laughing her head off.

"I'm…sorry…" she said in between bursts of laughter. "…Really, I am…I just…couldn't help it!" We walked back to camp. I was muttering revenge plots under my breath the whole way. As soon as we got back, I sat down on a log and resumed eating with Serrin.

"Oy, Zephyr, what happened to…"

"I don't want to talk about it." I sat in silence and ate. Then, a brilliant little scheme popped into my head. "Hey, Morn, do you have a knife I can borrow?" he handed me a blade, although he looked at me like I was nuts and scooted back several feet as soon as it was in my hands. I set off again in search of a piece of bark that would be just perfect for my plan…

Chapter 4
Lost and Found

Kimara leaped back in fear, screaming louder than seemed possible. I burst out laughing and took the mask down from my face.

I had gotten up very early that morning and hidden beside Kimara's tent, waiting to ambush her.

Me being the Halloween freak that I am, I thought up a frightening plan for revenge—a Zephyr specialty, if I may say. Last night, I had taken Morn's knife and found a piece of bark large enough to cover my face, carved a freakish design on it, and painted it up with juices from berries. It had taken me most of last night, which was fine with me, seeing that I have never been an early riser anyway.

Kimara gasped and panted for breath. She was backed up against a tree, eyeing me furiously. I was also panting for breath, but for a different reason entirely. Tears flooded my eyes from laughing so hard. I doubled over on the ground.

I laughed just about all morning long. Breakfast was a fairly simple meal, something I'd had before and dubbed "crevice world cereal". It consisted of clusters of some granola-like cereal suspended in dragon's milk (which tastes oddly like mint). Serrin was bouncing up and down to get started exploring for ruins, so the cooks had hardly had enough time to make even that much for breakfast.

"All right, then!" said Serrin, breakfast being officially over. "Zephyr, before we get started, I have something for you." he produced two items, one of which I recognized instantly; that was the sword I had used to destroy Ranook the first time I had been to the crevice world. He had used the help of several men unloading it from the APLEV, since the sword's enchantment assured that it was almost impossible to lift alone. For some reason, I was the only one who could wield it properly. It was tucked away in its sheath now, but I remembered its glittering, metallic blue blade, and the stone hilt that ended in a lion's head. I picked it up and carefully strapped it to my belt.

The second item was something I had never seen before. It was a piece of rock in a sort of oblong shape. It was a light, pale green and had chipped edges. Some kind of strange, almost hieroglyphic-like had been carved on the front. A hole had been put through it. Strung through the hole was a black cord tied in the back so as to make a pendant. I slipped it around my neck. "Where did this come from?" I said.

"It is a gift," replied Serrin, "carefully fashioned by the hands of Kimara and I, made of stone etched in the old language."

"What he means to say," interrupted Kimara, "is that the little shrine in that used to be in town which he dismantled for further study didn't come apart very easily. In fact, it chipped, so he had me help him turn it into a necklace to make it look intentional." Serrin winced and I knew her explanation must have struck home. The shrine she referred to (although I would have called it a really small temple) had their village laws written on it in some ancient language that Serrin was still deciphering, so he'd been forced to take it apart and make it mobile when we had to evacuate the village. Avoiding any further conversation on the subject, Serrin jumped up on a rock and began orchestrating the expedition.

"Everyone listen up!" He shouted. "We're going to divide up the search parties and scour the area for any trace of the ruins of a village. Old buildings, rusted utensils, scraps of cloth, artifacts, anything that could have once been part of the town. Organize yourselves into groups of four to six and scan the immediate area for anything. Report back here in half an hour!"

Serrin, Morn, Bednik, Kimara, and myself split into our own group and headed off into the woods. We passed by the pool and waterfall again, at which point Kimara began snickering. Watching her out of the corner of my eye, I resolved to find a really good way to scare her again sometime.

We shuffled off through the underbrush, ducked under tree branches, stumbled through weeds, and in general searched the area really well for the next twenty minutes. After that we just sat down and partook of some berries in a bowl with dragon's cream (made from dragon's milk) that Kimara had taken for herself when the cooks weren't looking. We sat down in the dirt, our backs against trees, passing the bowl around.

"Well," Morn sighed, his mouth full of the delectable treat. "Are you sure we're in the right place?" Serrin scratched his head and unrolled a parchment.

"Huh," he said quizzically. "Assuming my calculations are correct, absolutely. We should be right in the middle of the place. Maybe one of the other teams found something."

"Actually, I think I know the problem," piped up Kimara.

"Well, by all means then, tell us," responded Bednik, passing the bowl to her.

"Serrin said," she said in a scientific-sounding tone, "that we were in the right place *assuming his calculations were correct*. Knowing him, that's our problem right there." Her blue ponytail danced as she ducked the branch Serrin chucked in her general direction.

"I guess we'd better head back." I volunteered.

"All right," she said. "Lead the way."

"Me?" I said blankly.

"No, the tree behind you. Yes, you. You're supposed to be keeping track."

"What? Nobody told me that! I thought Bednik was going to do that!"

"No, that was Kimara's responsibility," said Bednik.

"I had thought Morn was gonna do it," offered Serrin.

"But you're the one with the map!" objected Morn. We all looked at each other a moment in silence.

"Yay," said Kimara with all the enthusiasm of a pile of a dead monkey. "We're lost."

"No," said Serrin. "We just don't know where we are." As the argument carried on in the background, something began clicking in my head. I was thinking back to the last time I had gotten lost in the crevice world. *How did he say it?* I thought. *"If you ever find that you need to get truly lost, just find me."* I leapt to my feet.

"We're not lost." I said. "His hut should be right around here somewhere." I began searching around.

"Who? What? Which hut?" asked Bednik.

"Tronks," I said simply, knowing they probably wouldn't understand what I meant anyway. Serrin, however, seemed to recognize the reference.

"I wish," he said. "Tronks is just an old folktale, Zephyr. He isn't real."

"I beg to differ," I said. "I've met him."

"You've met him?"

"Yeah."

"When?"

"Do you remember four years ago on the march to Ranook's castle? When I got separated from the rest of the group?" Serrin's jaw slowly edged itself open.

"But—but you couldn't have—I mean, it isn't..."

"Hate to interrupt this fascinating conversation, but who's Tronks?" said Kimara.

"He's a legendary folktale character," said Serrin, always the historian. "He appears only to people who are lost, and even then only occasionally."

"Well, I don't know if I'm exactly a legend, but my name is Tronks and you are all lost and therefore most certainly welcome into my humble home." We all turned to face the little man who was standing beside me, poking his head out from the door of a little hut. We all began laughing in surprise and relief.

"*Shh!* Silence!" he whispered furiously, the orange curls on his head bobbing. "Come inside, and be quick about it." Something was definitely wrong. The last time I had met him, he was constantly cheerful, even though the crevice world had been under a constant threat from living skeletons. As I stepped inside, I shuddered to think what could have possibly gotten him so concerned. Tronks carefully closed the door behind him.

We now stood in a candle-lit room with yellow walls graced by a large, continuous purple spiral. "Sorry about that," said Tronks. "There are some nasty characters about, and you can't be too careful."

"Nasty characters? Who?" Kimara nervously inquired. Tronks just shook his head, then pulled a watch out of his velvet coat.

"Oops! Would you look at that? It's time for dinner!" For some reason, he then felt it necessary to point to a random clock on the wall. Of course, you could probably point at any wall in the room and still be pointing at a clock—the walls were literally smothered in the devices.

"Dinnertime?" objected Bednik. "But it's hardly even afternoon yet!" Tronks checked another clock.

"Hmm, yes, you're right. It *is* 4 o'clock."

"What? But that's not what I…"

"Silly me," Tronks checked his pocket watch again. "It isn't either of those times! It's trippingtime!"

"Trippingtime?" said Morn. The last time I had visited Tronks, I had experienced what was called hattime. I was intensely curious as to what trippingtime possibly could be.

"Why, yes, trippingtime. It's when you must trip and fall as many times in as many ways as possible," declared the short, chubby Glunch. "Follow me." He set off into the next room and promptly tripped and fell flat on his stomach. I tripped over Tronks's couch on the way to the next room.

The next room was the kitchen, which was painted orange with green polka dots. A star-shaped table surrounded by octagonal chairs adorned the center of the room. Tronks continued through the room into the next room, tripping over a chair along the way. Bednik, who was beginning to get the idea, bumped into a wall and fell over.

The next room was decorated just as strangely as any of the other rooms in Tronks's house. Green and red candy cane style stripes covered the walls. A fireplace was on one wall. I tripped in a fantastic manner, spun in midair, slammed into the wall opposite me, and reeled backwards, stumbling over Tronks and knocking Kimara down in the process. Bednik then tripped over me and Kimara, somersaulted forward, and crashed into the wall. Tronks was grinning from ear to ear now that people had caught on.

Things continued like this for the next several minutes until Serrin, always eager to find the ruins, decided to question Tronks about them. "Tronks," he said, clearing his throat. "You know what we were doing when we got lost? We were searching for a third village built by the brother of Panok and Shanar. I was wondering if perhaps you just might know something about it."

"Ah, yes, Yoen," Tronks sighed, falling over backwards. "His village is difficult to find. I'm not surprised you haven't found it, though it was under your nose all along."

"What?" said Serrin eagerly. "You know where it is?" Tronks just smiled, got up, and left the room. Serrin scrambled after him. Kimara, Bednik, Morn, and I disentangled ourselves and followed them into the living room, where Tronks held open the door and ushered us outside into a narrow cave.

Chapter 5
The Lost Village

"Of course!" Serrin said. "It's underground!"

"It really was under our noses!" marveled Kimara. I turned around to thank Tronks, but the Glunch was already gone—and so was any trace of his hut.

The cave was lit with lanterns that I assumed were fueled by magic. We proceeded deeper underground as the tunnel slanted downwards. Before long, we found ourselves at a crossroads.

"Well, which way do we go?" asked Morn.

"To tell you the truth, I don't think it really matters," responded Serrin. So we just went straight ahead. Before long, we came to another crossroads.

"Hold on a minute," said Serrin. "It looks like this little place has been built in blocks." Time would prove Serrin both right and wrong. He was right in that the passages had been constructed around square blocks. He was wrong, however, in calling the place little. As we wandered around for what seemed like ages, we discovered that not only were there endless webs of hallways, but in between those hallways had been homes and huts carved into the rock, fully furnished but deserted.

We traversed the mazelike passages for what felt like an eternity. Finally, we found ourselves in a larger main hallway about fifteen feet across and twenty feet high. "Here we go," said Serrin. "This looks like it goes somewhere. Let's follow it." And we ended up following this passage for a really long time.

So I found some paper and started writing this tale to pass the time and now I'm finishing it and we're still stuck in this stupid passage. Just kidding. Actually, it went on for about five minutes and then curved sharply to the right. There it bridged out over a vast expanse of nothingness. Huge, cavernous rock walls surrounded the side. In the middle, at the end of the bridge, was a pedestal.

Not knowing what else to do, we crossed the bridge toward the pedestal. The rock bridge was plenty stable, but it was a dizzying journey nonetheless. One step too far to either side and you were a goner.

Fortunately, we crossed the gap without incident. On the other side, we discovered that the pedestal had faded writing on it. It looked vaguely familiar, although I couldn't read it. Serrin, however, had no trouble reading it—it was the old language he'd studied for so long. He knelt down in front of it. Brushing the dust off the pedestal, he concentrated for several moments, then spoke aloud. "On this pedestal will lie…until it falls to the open sky." Kimara peered at him in bewilderment.

"What?" she said after several moments.

"That's what it says." he replied. "Or at least the parts I can make out." We stood there utterly bewildered for several moments.

"Well, now what?" said Kimara with a huge sigh.

"Hold on a moment…" said Serrin. "There's something here…a switch or something…" I heard a *click* and a stone grinding noise. The top of the stone pedestal opened up. The lid was split down the middle. Each half swung open opposite the other. Inside the pedestal was a red metallic liquid. I had seen something similar once before. In Ranook's castle there had been a well filled with metallic blue liquid that perfectly matched the blade of my sword. When weapons came in contact with the liquid, it caused them to color the same shade of blue and gave them a special ability—the ability to kill the Undead, who had been almost invincible.

It was for this reason that I decided to dip my sword in the liquid as an experiment. The color of the blade seemed to shimmer before my eyes. Then the familiar blue color gave way to a metallic purple.

"What did…" Kimara never finished her sentence. The platform began trembling. We felt the stone under our feet kick up as the darkness receded away below us. A rushing wind hit me in the face. Suddenly we shot up through the ground to the surface. The shock sent me tumbling off the platform. I landed on something soft, then felt something slam onto me like a bag on cement. Dirt rained down for several seconds. Then the shower stopped and I could see again. Except the only thing I saw was blue. "Wow, that was a lot better of a landing than I expected," said Kimara from on top of me.

"That's because you landed on me, not the ground," I said in a strained voice.

"Oh well," she said casually and leapt up, waltzing away and whistling, thoroughly unshaken. Serrin and I picked ourselves up. A few feet away, Morn and Bednik did the same. The platform we had been standing on was now protruding several feet from the ground. We paused a moment to observe this before following Kimara into the woods.

Chapter 6
Empty World

It would be safe to say that the first thing we noticed upon arriving back at camp was that it was completely deserted. We stood still in the midst of camp for several moments before I piped up, "Where is everyone?"

"Maybe they're still out looking." offered Kimara.

"I told them to meet back here after half an hour. We've probably been longer," said Serrin.

"Maybe they're out looking for us then."

"Maybe." he sat down on a log to await the arrival of the others. I looked around through the trees into the mist.

We must have been there for several minutes while we waited for the others to return. It seemed like forever, lying there on the ground and waiting. Finally Serrin leapt up.

"Something's not right," he said. No sooner did he finish the sentence than Gorlub and Bulrog appeared through the fog in tattered clothing.

"Serrin!" I shouted, catching his attention. I pointed over to Gorlub and Bulrog. A grim expression caught his face.

"I knew it," he groaned.

"Hey there!" yelled Morn. "What happened?"

"Something…" panted Bulrog. "Something attacked us back there…something big…"

"It got the rest of our party," added Gorlub.

"We'd better get to the APLEV," said Kimara. "That way if it attacks us we'll be ready to fight it…or ready to run." Following her suggestion, we scurried away to the safety of the wooden platform and spent the next several minutes huddled near the seat of the APLEV, prepared to take off at any second if need be.

After a while, we decided that whatever had attacked everyone else was not going to come after us. However, we couldn't think of anything to do, so we just sat there for a while longer. Finally, Morn suggested that we head back to one of the villages and regroup into search parties with the villagers.

We fired up the APLEV and drove most of the way to Shanar in silence. The field gnomes did not bother us. In fact, they seemed to have disappeared with everyone else.

When we finally arrived at the seaside village, we were greeted by another nasty surprise: the village was deserted as well.

We were dumbfounded. Somehow, everyone in the crevice world, except for the seven of us, had disappeared. It was impossible. It felt like a dream world. I sat down in shock in the shade of a rakahn tree. Rakahn was a kind of fruit unique to the crevice world. Kimara plopped down next to me, eyes widened and mouth agape. She was clearly in shock. I couldn't blame her.

"How did this *happen?*" she said in a weak voice. She was about to cry.

"I don't even know *what* happened, much less how," I replied.

Gorlub and Bulrog had chosen to wander around in a state of complete shock. Serrin was sitting on a barrel near a shop. Bednik and Morn had collapsed in the shade of another tree (which didn't provide much shade since the weather was foggy anyway) and were lying on the grass, staring into the clouds. I looked again at Serrin. Then I saw the sign on the shop he was sitting by. It was the Jokes & Fireworks Factory. I smiled sadly as three laughing little faces slid into my mind as if to mock me with their silent laughter. Trying to push the toddlers' faces out of my head, I stood up to stretch. Still the memories flooded into my head. Memories of happy children and hide-and-seek games on ships; memories of sticks and stones being playfully thrown; and above all, the memory of death rearing its ugly face to leer at me.

The scream caused me to jolt to my senses. Whirling around, I drew my sword on instinct. It had been a male voice. Then I noticed that Gorlub and Bulrog were missing. Serrin and I took off running at full speed towards where the noise had come from. We entered a hut that I recognized as the one shared by Gorlub and Bulrog. My eyes quickly scanned over the messy half that Bulrog occupied and the neat half that Gorlub owned before noticing the wall. On it had been scrawled two words: *Ranook's Castle*. Gorlub and Bulrog stood next to it, mouths hanging open.

"What happened?" asked Serrin.

"W-We just thought we'd check back home for supplies…" said Gorlub.

"And we came in and found *this* on the wall," finished Bulrog. I stepped closer and inspected the wall. The writing looked like charcoal. It looked like it had been freshly done. I sheathed my sword and whirled around to face them. "This means there's someone left besides us," I said. Then I noticed them staring in fear at me like they had been staring at the wall. "What?" I said. Serrin blinked and rubbed his eyes.

"I…you just…popped out of nowhere, mate. I guess I just didn't see you there."

"Whether you saw me or not, that looks fresh, and the person who did it might be around here still. Let's spread out and search." We all bolted from the hut in separate directions. I took to the back roads and hidden alleys between the buildings. My search results yielded nothing, so I retreated back to the rakahn tree and found the others already waiting for me. I shook my head to show I'd found nothing.

"Well, now what?" inquired Bednik.

"Isn't it obvious?" said Kimara. "We go to Ranook's castle. Somebody obviously wants us there."

"But what if it's a trap?" asked Morn.

"It's *obviously* a trap," I said. "We'll just have to be prepared."

"It's likely the only way we'll ever get to the bottom of this," added Kimara.

"I'm with the girl," said Bulrog. "We should go to the castle." Gorlub shot him a funny look. "Even though we'll probably all die," he added under his breath.

"It's settled, then," said Serrin. "To the APLEV."

"Hold on," I said. "Did you guys ever get a new ship after the old one blew up?" Gorlub pointed out toward the sea, where a set of sails was visible. "We'll take that, then. We can carry more supplies on it, including the APLEV."

"Well, I guess *that* settles it," said Serrin.

Chapter 7
Sea of Death

It was fairly smooth sailing. We had loaded the ship with supplies in Shanar, then set sail with the APLEV on board. Everyone else pretty much had the sailing and navigation covered, so I decided to sit back and sharpen my sword. I had found the materials to do so in the cargo hold of the ship.

As I sat grinding my blade against the stone, Bulrog walked up and leaned against the mast I was sitting next to. He casually glanced around, then pulled something out of a pocket and looked at it. His hand was at just the right angle so I could not see what it was. He seemed fixated on the object, though, whatever it was.

"Whatcha got there?" I asked. He snapped to his senses and crammed the object into his pocket.

"Where did *you* come from?" he demanded.

"I've been here the whole time," I said.

"Wait a minute…you keep slipping out of focus…it's like my eyes don't want to see you."

"Gee, thanks."

"No, I mean…put down your sword." Staring at him like he was nuts, I obeyed. "Huh," he said. "Now I see you fine." I picked up the sword again. "Now I'm having trouble seeing you. It's like you're blending in." I was starting to get excited.

"Now *that* is a nifty trick," I said. "Kimara! Over here!" Hearing my shout, she walked over from the edge of the ship to where I was. A frown crossed her face as she looked around.

"I thought Zephyr called me," she said. Bulrog shrugged. I sneaked around behind her and sheathed my sword. Finally she decided that she had been hearing things and turned to walk back. That's when she saw me and screamed.

"It works!" I said excitedly to Bulrog. A broad smile appeared on his face.

"I bet the ship sinks and we all die!" he said enthusiastically before walking off. I ran off to find Serrin, leaving Kimara alone and thoroughly bewildered. My head was already filled with useful applications for this new talent. I realized that the sword must have been given the ability to blend into its surroundings when it came in contact with the red liquid we had found in the town of Yoen. This was even more of an advantage than the sword's ability to kill the Undead.

Suffice it to say that I spent the next half-hour or so having fun by driving everyone insane. I would disappear whenever I was needed and watch everyone tear the ship apart looking for me. Then I would reappear right in the middle of the deck and claim to have been there the whole time. It was terribly amusing watching everyone go stark raving nuts.

After infuriating everyone on the ship, I decided to put away the stuff I was using to sharpen my sword. I was tucking the stone away under a cloth when I noticed something glinting in the corner. I walked over to the object. It was a mirror. It had been tucked away behind some old crates and trunks that were covered with cobwebs and dust. The mirror was an intricate piece of art. Although the glass itself was a little foggy, the border was made of what appeared to be a collection of miniature skulls. I noticed that although the floor the mirror had been lying on had thick layers of dust, the mirror itself had virtually no dust on it. This meant that the mirror had been placed here recently. I grasped it in my hand. It was just small enough to fit in my hand without being seen from the other side. My mind instantly jumped to the object I had seen Bulrog holding on the deck about an hour ago.

I had no idea if it really belonged to Bulrog or not, but the point was that someone had placed it there recently. Judging by Bulrog's flustered reaction, the object was probably something he was not supposed to have.

I'm not the smartest guy in the world, but I'm smart enough to figure out that if someone is trying to hide something, and that something turns out to be a mirror lined with skulls, that's probably not a good sign. I was trying to figure out what to do with the mirror when I heard footsteps coming down the stairs behind me. I dropped the mirror into a pile of sacks in the middle of the large room and drew my sword, ducking into the shadows to ensure my invisibility. Kimara jumped the last several stairs and landed with a solid *thud* on the wooden floor. She peered around to make sure nobody else was there, then peered carefully at an object tucked into her hand. My eyes snapped toward the pile of sacks in the middle of the room. *What if there was more than one of those things?* She glanced around once more, then looked at her palm again, then started walking. *She was headed straight for the pile of sacks I'd put the mirror in.* I held my breath. Something was very wrong here. Then she neatly skirted around the pile and went to a shelf on the other side of the room. I started breathing again. She checked over her shoulder once more, then pulled a box off the shelf. Whatever she was doing, she didn't want anyone to see. The box was wood and had some kind of writing on it, but it was too far away for me to read. She placed the object in her hand on the shelf. Putting her fingers into a tiny crack between the box and the lid, she began prying the lid off. It gave a sharp *pop* as it went flying through the air. Her hand went into the box and came out with a scone in it.

A scone. I had totally freaked out over what turned out to be Kimara grabbing a scone. Then the door to the cargo hold banged open. Moving with incredible speed, Kimara shoved the scone into her mouth, slid the box back on the shelf, and grabbed whatever it was she'd put on the shelf. As the footsteps shuffled down the staircase, Kimara frantically searched for a hiding place. Right as two pairs of legs came into view, she made a dash for it. She was heading straight for me.

Chapter 8
Puzzle Pieces

Kimara came rolling into the corner, nearly colliding with me. The back of her head was not two inches from my nose. As the two figures descended into the cargo hold, I came to the sudden realization that she still didn't know I was here. Trying to steady my erratic breathing, I focused on the figures now in the cargo hold. They were Serrin and Bednik. I peered over the blue ponytail that now partially blocked my view.

"What are we doing tonight, then?" said Bednik.

"I was thinking mashed potatoes with a touch of garlic." replied Serrin.

"Let's add a touch of rakahn juice to wash that down."

"Excellent idea."

How is it, I thought to myself, *that girls' hair always, always, always, ALWAYS smells so good?* It is a mystery that still haunts me to this day.

Anyway, Serrin and Bednik went about plucking items off of various shelves for that night's dinner. Eventually, they got around to the shelf that Kimara had been at. "Ah, nuts," said Serrin.

"What's the matter?" asked Bednik.

"Some rascal's nabbed one of the scones I was going to use for breakfast tomorrow."

"Same one who's been munching into all the vittles, I bet," Bednik replied darkly. It was as he said this that I finally realized I could see what Kimara was holding. It was sort of a greenish color, as if the color had tinted with age. The surface was covered with strange writing of some sort. It looked very familiar.

"That everything, then?"

"Yeah, probably. Let's haul this lot up to the deck and cook it."

I had figured out why the chunk of stone looked familiar. It closely resembled the necklace I was wearing. The necklace had come from a chip off the temple wall, so it was safe to say that the chunk of stone in her hand had the same origin. By this time Serrin and Bednik had left with the ingredients for the night's meal. Kimara waited a minute before following them up.

After she was gone, I sheathed my sword and stepped out of the shadows, once again visible to the naked eye. The first thing I did was retrieve the mirror. I had several questions burning to be answered, but first I had to decide what I was going to do with this evil-looking object. I didn't want to leave it in the cargo hold in case Bulrog (assuming that was whom it belonged to) came back to retrieve it. However, I was afraid to keep it on me. Who knew what kind of magical side effects the thing could have? I decided to keep it on me for now and find a good hiding spot on the deck later.

On the way out of the cargo hold, I noticed a large object covered by a sheet near the stairs. My curiosity got the better of me. It turned out to be the dismantled wall of the temple I had seen when I first came to the crevice world. It was indeed chipped and cracked in several places. However, this did not explain why Kimara had a piece of it in her possession.

By the time I made it to the deck, it was near dusk. I was put to work almost immediately helping

Serrin mash potatoes. I must admit that I am not a big fan of work, but it wasn't that bad, since he kept me company.

When I had finished with the potatoes, I decided to take a stroll in the cool night air. I found Kimara on the deck. She was relaxing in a corner, staring at something in her palm.

"What's that?" I said, nodding at her hand, even though I knew what the answer would be. What I really wanted to know was why she had it. She held out her palm so I could see. Sure enough, it was the chunk from the temple wall.

"Serrin had a few of these," she said. "He decided to ask some of us for help. He's been sharing his notes with us, but I still can't make heads or tails of it." A sudden thought dawned on me.

"Did Bulrog get one?"

"Yeah, why?"

"I saw him with something, but he tried to hide it from me."

"Yeah, that's Bulrog. He got one and tried to decipher it, but he hates to be seen with the thing. It's almost educational, so he prefers not to be associated with it."

I was almost disappointed that the incident with Bulrog was so easily explained. This meant that I still had to find the culprit who owned the mirror.

I chitchatted with Kimara for a while, then hastily excused myself. I decided to hide the mirror between some barrels on the bow.

After that I took a trip up to the crow's nest, where I prefer to spend my voyages. The imposing outline of Ranook's castle lay not too far off, silhouetted against the moon. It was getting harder to see, though; it was being obscured by clouds. There was a definite chill in the air. It could mean only one thing: storm's coming.

Chapter 9
Rough Seas and Rougher Roads

It was worse than we anticipated. Ten-foot-tall waves slammed into the side of the ship, spraying us with salt water and tilting the boat precariously. It was difficult to find footing on the slick deck. The last time I had been in the crevice world, I had encountered shraks, which were a lot like sharks, only more colorful. I was not eager to repeat the experience.

Kimara did not like storms and had gone below where it was drier, although she was still being tossed violently. I was helping Serrin turn the wheel. It took two fit people just to move it in the wind. We were struggling to stay on course as it was and the blinding flashes of lightning and loud peals of thunder were not helping. Bulrog and Gorlub were taking care of the tangled mess that used to be our sails. Bednik and Morn were taking care of navigation, although Morn kept having to go below to check the supplies and Kimara.

Yet another wave smashed into the bow. The ship rocked violently and I slipped on the deck. I held on tightly to the wheel as the raging sea came into view beneath my feet. The ship was tilted all the way over on its side. I was hanging on to the wheel, my body at the same angle as the ship.

Then it came crashing back down onto its belly. I tumbled back onto the deck and slid across it for a moment.

"HOW MUCH CLOSER ARE WE?" I yelled to Morn.

"WHAT?" came the reply.

"HOW MUCH CLOSER ARE WE?" I repeated.

"I DON'T KNOW!" That was not the most comforting thing to hear. Then again, it was hard enough to see the other side of the ship in this weather.

A bolt of lightning flew by the mast and splashed into the water.

"I don't know if this is safe!" shouted Serrin. "We'd better get below!" a massive tidal wave rose up over the ship. I braced myself. The wave cascaded onto the ship's deck. The force alone smashed me down onto the deck. I was helpless for a moment. Everything was pitch black. There was no sound. The only things that existed were the ship's wheel and the force trying to pull me away from it into oblivion.

Then I came up gasping for air as the water slid away off the deck. "There's nothing we can do!" yelled Morn. "It's too strong! Get below!" Having said this, he immediately ran for the door that led below the deck. A brilliant flash of lightning illuminated this move. Then came the clap of thunder. And with the clap of thunder came another sound. It was a scream.

The thunder was so close to the lightning that the light was still there as I whirled around. Everyone was looking toward the mast, where the scream had come from.

It seemed to happen in slow motion. The limp figure fell from the mast, tumbling like a rag doll. I slid over to the rail of the ship as if to catch him, but there was nothing I could do. His trajectory led him straight overboard into the raging sea. I had to just sit there and watch the limp form of Gorlub be washed away under the water, shocked expression frozen permanently on his face. I sat there and stared for a moment longer before I was pulled away by Serrin.

Everyone made it into the cargo hold safely with the exception of Gorlub. From there we entered a hallway that led to a couple of cabins. These were the only spaces down here besides the cargo hold.

We huddled into the cabin that Kimara was in. It churned and rocked with the waves. The single lantern that lit it was being buffeted around on the chain that held it to the ceiling. Bulrog was terribly upset. He banged his fist on the wall in fury.

"What's wrong?" asked Kimara. Silence filled the cabin for a moment.

"We lost Gorlub." I said quietly. Kimara' s eyes widened. Her mouth opened as if to say something, but she thought better of it and closed it again. Her eyes started to water over. She seemed to be in shock as she leaned over into my side.

I couldn't blame her. I was having trouble with the concept of Gorlub being dead myself. The events of the last two minutes felt like some sort of bizarre dream. Bulrog sat in the corner under the blanket and grumbled to himself. I wasn't really listening to what he was saying. I was too cold and tired.

Somehow, despite the peals of thunder and the constant jolting of the ship, I managed to slip into the grasp of sleep.

Chapter 10
Amber Skies

Indeed, I actually found myself wondering if last night's events actually were a dream in the morning. I awoke in a pitch black cabin. I guess the light finally must have flickered out while we slept.

I managed to find my way to the door, although I think I stumbled over Bulrog in the process. The hallway was quite dark as well. My vision had adjusted a bit, though. I made my way into the cargo hold. A small shaft of amber light was emanating through the crack under the door. I crawled up the stairs (tripping on the stairs in the dark is no fun) and opened the door.

As soon as my eyes adjusted, the first thing I noticed was the sky. It was no longer blue. The sky had somehow turned amber. The clouds that floated in front of it took on a slightly darker tint than the light amber that was now the sky. My first thought was that it was a trick of the early morning light. Nearby I found a large splinter that I used as a measure of the time. Judging by the shadow it cast, the time was somewhere in the vicinity of noon. After I did that trick I was feeling clever and resourceful until I realized I could have just looked at my own shadow.

The next thing I took into account was the landscape. We were no longer at sea. The landscape was that of a marsh. Rivers and streams crisscrossed the islands of reeds like errant bolts of lightning. The streams could not be very deep since we had run aground in one of them. The scenery went on for several thousand feet before abruptly turning into a wooded slope. A little off to my right, it met a different fate. It was still a slope, but instead of trees, this hill was covered in golden fields of wheat that rippled with the wind.

The light from the sky didn't seem to affect the color of everything else. Everything seemed a little off color, but not too much. Whatever this place was, it was unlike any place I had ever seen in the crevice world before. We were someplace new.

It was after this dawned on me that I took a look around and noticed something else on one of the hills. It was a house. I couldn't tell too much about it from here, but I could see that it was very large. It appeared to have something similar to Tudor-style architecture. I wondered how I could have missed it. It stood out plainly at the top of the hill of wheat and meadows.

I turned around and faced the open sea. There was really nothing else to do until everyone else was up. Hopefully Serrin would have some idea where we were.

As it turned out, the first person on the deck was Bulrog. Bulrog yawned and scratched, then glanced around. He saw the sky and did a double-take, rubbing his eyes.

"Good, so I'm not the only one who sees it," I said.

"Yeah," said Bulrog gruffly. "I was worried something was wrong with my eyes for a moment there."

"Me too. What do you think is causing it?"

"No idea. Probably better off not thinking about it." We stared at the sky a moment longer. "Oh, that reminds me. There was something Gorlub wanted you to have."

He ran below for a moment, then returned with a coffin-shaped box about four feet long. He slid the box over to me unceremoniously, then returned to frowning at the sky.

I took the lid off the box. Inside was a bunch of crepe paper wrapped around something. On top of the paper was a note.

```
Zephyr-
I have been making this in case
you need it. It is very valuable
and can only be used once, so DO
NOT UNWRAP IT UNLESS YOU ARE
IN REAL TROUBLE. It is not yet
finished, but it should be very
potent. If you are reading this
note, it means that I have not
been able to give it to you in
person. I have been suspecting
that I might have to leave
suddenly for some time now, so I
am writing this in case I am
right. Please keep this with you
and heed my warning.
-Gorlub
```

I pondered the note for a while. What did it mean? Had Gorlub somehow foreseen his death? What was the object and what was it for? I was severely tempted to go ahead and open the paper, but I decided to heed Gorlub's warning. I put the lid back on the box. The note was uncharacteristically un-cheery for Gorlub. Something was going on, but I wasn't sure what.

Bulrog and I elected to pretend that the sky was normal when everyone else came on deck. This drove people stark raving nuts.

After everyone else was on deck and we had clearly established that the sky was not blue, we had to go about deciding on our next course of action. Eventually we settled on checking out the house on the hill.

To begin our journey, we had to climb down the side of the ship into the river. It was only a few feet deep, but the current was swift. I rolled up the legs of my pants as we treaded water. Each step any of us made was met with a resounding splash.

After several minutes of working our way upstream, we stopped to rest on a sandbar that rose up to interrupt the stream. We were all quite comfortable until we felt the small rumbling underneath us. It was slowly growing more intense. "What's that?" asked Kimara, voicing the question we were all thinking. Her question was quickly answered as the mound exploded into a million pieces of dirt and sent us all flying into the air.

As I landed facedown in the water, I managed to snap my head up quickly enough to catch a glimpse of what was happening; something had come up out of the mound. Something big. It appeared to be a big pile of mustard-colored stones. Then, as it unfolded itself, I realized it was alive. It was a giant man made of rocks. The beast threw back its head and let out a mighty roar. "I don't think it's friendly!" yelled Morn. He was right. Kimara rolled out of the way just in time as the rock monster smashed down his huge fist. We ran for our lives. The monster let out a growl and chased after us.

We began ducking off into side streams in an effort to shake it off. It didn't work. The rock monster stuck doggedly to our path. Then we caught our lucky break. A canoe had run aground against a sandbar, complete with paddles. I grabbed it as we ran by and jerked hard to pull it free. The current was now pushing behind us, so it would be easier to outrun the monster. I jumped in and everyone else followed. Morn and I took the paddles. He was in the rear and I was in the front, so it was much easier to outmaneuver the creature.

A few minutes later, we were floating safely towards shore. "Well, we could have done without that," said Bednik.

"Wait a moment," interjected Kimara. "Do you remember being bothered by field gnomes on the way to Shanar?"

"No," said Morn. "Or anything else for that matter."

"Exactly. It was empty all the way. No birds, no creatures, no insects."

"And?" said Bulrog.

"And we were just attacked by something. I don't know what it was, but it was obviously alive."

"Well, wherever we are, we're not where we were, which means whatever happened where we were may not have happened where we are, wherever we are," said Serrin. Everyone turned to stare at him. "In other words, there may be creatures here that weren't affected by the people wherever we came from."

The train of thought was derailed when the canoe bumped into solid ground. We disembarked. We were on a dirt path that twisted up the hill to the house. The path was rough and uneven and kept turning this way and that without rhyme or reason until it reached the house.

At the end of the path were a few wooden
steps that led up to a very nice wooden patio. It was
much easier to admire the Tudor architecture from
here. The house was very large and elaborately built.
A small greenhouse protruded from the left side.
Above the door was a sign that stated simply,
"Tookie".

"Who or what is Tookie?" I asked.

"I've no idea," said Bednik. "Perhaps the owner
of the house?"

"Let's see if anyone's home." said Kimara. She
knocked on the door. Nothing happened. She
knocked harder this time. Still nothing happened. She
let a minute or two pass, then tried the door. It was
open. We cautiously ventured inside.

"Hello?" yelled Serrin. There was no response.

We were in a hallway with white walls and a
white ceiling. Wooden beams supported the walls.
The door had opened into the side of the hallway, so
there were two choices as to where to go. We went
left.

We ended up in what appeared to be a living
room. A wooden bowl of crackers sat unattended on
the table. On the left was a window that provided a
view of the amber sky outside. The walls of this room
matched those of the hallway. The floor was a very
smooth looking polished wood of a light color. A sofa
had been stitched together out of various types of
materials and was sitting next to the table. On the
table next to the crackers was a piece of parchment
and a quill. The parchment had been scribbled on a
good deal. There was a sketch of the monster we had
encountered in the streams next to the scribbling. The
scribbling read like this:

Gochakra-Monster that buries itself in the sand

*to await its victims. Eats meat occasionally, but
mostly prefers rocks and dirt.
Usually seen near the ocean, despite the fact
that they are afraid of water.*

I was so interested in this that I almost didn't notice everyone else had left. I went into the next room looking for them. The next room turned out to be the greenhouse.

The greenhouse contained many types of rare and exotic plants which I had never seen before. Under each plant was a sign with the plant's name. There was a particularly interesting plant that reminded one of a large Venus flytrap. It had long, thorny vines that reached up to the ceiling and numerous sets of vicious-looking jaws. I never got a good look at the name, since the nameplate had a clean bite mark straight through the middle.

Shuffling my way through the collection of overgrown greenery, I eventually found the center of the greenhouse. In the middle of everything was a small clearing of worn-out stone floor. In the middle of the clearing stood a stone pedestal. On the pedestal stood a worn statue of a cherub. The whole thing was overgrown with ivy and vines.

At the base of the pedestal was a book. The book had been dropped suddenly, by the looks of it. It was splayed out on the ground. The title was clearly visible on the spine. The book was called *Dark Magic.* The subtitle was *A Glossary of Dark Magic Items and Their Uses.* All of a sudden I felt a lot less comfortable in the home of this Tookie person. I looked again at the angle of the book. It did indeed look like someone had dropped it. In fact, it almost seemed as if someone had seen me coming and dropped it. The hairs on the back of my neck stood up. Ever so carefully, I bent over and picked it up. I froze when I saw what was on the page. It was a drawing of a very familiar-looking mirror. A mirror with skulls surrounding the edge of it. The same mirror I had seen on the ship. The description was even more chilling.

Dark Mirror
The Dark Mirror is a device used to keep in touch with someone (i.e., a trusted servant to their Dark master).
It can also be used to spy on someone by transmitting visual information to the holder of the other mirror.
These items always come in pairs. Only the two members of the pair can link to each other.

What had someone been doing with one of these on the ship? Who had placed it there?
I slowly lowered the book. Two cold gray eyes were staring me in the face.

Chapter 11
Tookie

At first I jumped back and dropped the book. Then I realized it was just the statue of the cherub. That thing was really creepy. I drew my sword for invisibility just in case.

Moving as quickly as I could, I picked up the book and swiftly departed through the maze of plants. I finally found my way to another doorway. This one led to a kitchen.

The kitchen had a long counter down the middle. Cooking utensils hung up over the counter. On either side of the room were cupboards and more counters. To my left a window looked out over rolling hills and valleys. A stone path extended down from the side of the house into one of the valleys.

Turning my attention back to the kitchen, I noticed the collection of recipe books sitting on the counter. All of the books advertised tropical, foreign, or unusual titles on their spines.

To my right was a doorway leading to the living room. Straight ahead was another hallway. I took the hallway.

The first door in the hallway was on my right. It opened into...a bathroom. That was pretty advanced for the crevice world. It even had a stone toilet (with no water—it was one of the old medieval kinds) and a mirror. The whole thing was topped off with a stone sink and a bar of soap. It looked like the sink might even have running water.

As fascinating as the bathroom was, I was looking for the others at the moment and was not interested in further investigating it. I returned to the hallway and ducked into the door on the left. It was just a storage closet. I continued farther down the hall and into another door on the right.

The well-worn desk and piles of parchment announced that this was the study. A lantern hung by means of a chain from the ceiling. Two smaller lanterns sat on either side of the desk. Various chairs were cluttered around the room, although most of them were being used as holding spaces for piles of books, writing supplies, telescopes, devices of mathematical use, and what have you.

However, I heard the murmur of conversation coming from the next room, so that was where I went next. As it turned out, the next room was larger than any before it. This was the library. Bookshelves extended a full two stories high. Amber light poured in from a skylight on the roof. Comfy chairs adorned a rug in the middle of the room.

It was in the chairs that I found what I was looking for. Serrin and Kimara sat in the chairs, deep in conversation, books open on their laps.

"Sorry to interrupt," I said. "But where is everybody?"

"Bulrog went outside," said Kimara. "He said something about the potential for education being too thick to breathe in here, whatever that means."

"Morn and Bednik went upstairs to investigate," added Serrin. "Look what I found! It's a history of our part of the world! Whoever lives here knows about our part of the world, but we didn't know about them."

Only mildly interested by this observation, I found my way up some stairs at the end of the hall. Upstairs I found a bedroom with a storage closet and stone bathtub, a room with a fireplace and some paintings, and a spiral staircase that led upward. I took the staircase.

I ended up in a tower that appeared to be serving as an observatory. A window was on either side. Astronomy charts lined the walls. Dusty old trunks sat unopened in corners. Against one window was a telescope. Morn and Bednik were huddled over the telescope.

"Ah, Zephyr," said Morn. "You're just in time. Look through here and tell me what you see."

The telescope was focused on the town. I saw nothing besides that, though. No inhabitants. No people in the street doing business.

"It's deserted," I said.

"Exactly," he said. "So we can only presume that whatever happened in our land happened here as well. However, that does not explain why these creatures still remain." He pointed out the other window at the rock creatures, or Gochakra, who were now walking about somewhat clumsily amongst the streams and rivers we had come through to get here.

"Good point," I said. "It also does not explain why we are still here. Tronks also survived."

"Tronks I can explain," said Bednik. "He doesn't play by the rules. His house always seems to be in a constant state of limbo. It's always switching location. Perhaps that's what saved him."

"And us," I said. Bednik nodded.

"Still doesn't explain the creatures," Morn said.

"They're called Gochakra," I explained. "I read a paper about them downstairs. They eat meat occasionally, but mostly prefer rocks and dirt. They bury themselves in the sand to sleep."

"Wait a minute!" exclaimed Morn. "That's it!"

"What's it?" I said.

"They bury themselves in the sand. They're underground. Do you remember where the village of Yoen was?"

"Underground," I said. "Just like them. Anyone who is underground when whatever happened happens isn't affected." This explanation satisfied them, but there was something nagging at the back of my head; some unsatisfied hole in the theory. Before I had time to think it over, however, Bednik began talking.

"Now we know why we were spared," he said. "What we don't know is what exactly happened and who did it."

"And why," I added. "I think we can safely reason that something like this could not have happened on its own. Someone must have done it. Someone who had a good reason."

"Here's an idea," interjected Morn. "What if we were meant to survive? What if someone wanted us here?"

"To use us as game pieces on a playing board." It was a chilling thought, and certainly a valid one. Judging by the instructions to go to Ranook's castle, whoever had done this wanted the showdown on their own turf.

"Wait," I said, a sudden thought coming to me. "How are we going to get to Ranook's castle now?" Morn shrugged.

"We're not, I guess. The ship was pretty well lodged in there. We'll just have to get everyone together to reassess the situation." Then he looked at my hand and frowned. Following his glance, I realized I was still holding the book I'd found in the greenhouse. I handed it over for him to look at.

"Found it in the greenhouse," I said. Morn just raised one eyebrow and handed it back.

"He's taking it hard," said Bednik. He had
moved over to the window and was looking out. I
moved over to him and followed his sightline. Bulrog
was sitting alone on the patio watching the Gochakra.
"He won't show it, but he is."

I had been so busy the last few hours I had
almost forgotten about Gorlub's death. Not being able
to think of anything to say, I just allowed a moment of
silence and left.

Kimara was alone in the library when I got
back, so I took Serrin's seat. She said that he had
taken a large stack of books and moved to the study
to search for quills and parchment to make notes with.
I told her what we had deduced in the tower. She was
only half listening to me, as she had found an
interesting book about physics to read.

I began flipping through random entries in *Dark
Magic* to see if I could find anything useful. The first
entry looked like this:

Dark Oracle

Although putting this first violates the
alphabetical order rule, this must go
first since it the definitive Dark Object.
It rules the pecking order.
Said to exist on a plane of its own, the
Dark Oracle is like a god. It feeds off the
power of those who serve it. It is
powerful enough to alter reality when
backed with enough support. The
Undead and other such creatures do not
add to its power since they have no soul.
The Dark Oracle is a sinister version of
the Oracle. The Oracle itself is often
credited with the creation of the world. It
is commonly accepted that everything has

a light side and a dark side; the Oracle
split itself in two so it would not have an
evil side. Instead of the intended result,
the Dark Oracle was created.

"HEY!" Kimara's shout made me jump.
"What?"
"I said your name about four times. Aren't you
paying attention?"
"What? Oh, yeah, I just…got lost in my book."
"Oh. Well, I just read some neat stuff about
hydraulic pressure." And she plopped back down in
her chair without another peep. Somewhat confused
as to what that was all about, I flipped to another
random entry in the book.

BRANDING
A practice used by Dark Masters on their
servants. When a servant is especially
well trusted, their master will cast a spell
on them that burns the image of a skull
on their chest. This symbolizes that the said
person has chosen the path of destruction,
as well as the strong trust between master
and servant.

I flipped to another entry, toward the back this
time.

PLACEHOLDING
This is considered to be a Dark Spell due
to the sheer immorality of it. It is not
necessarily so when performed on with the
permission of the receiving party, but this is
very rarely obtained first.
At a particular point when traveling

between two worlds, the traveler is in a state of limbo that allows him to be switched with someone else. This spell will transport a duplicate of someone that is actually not that person into the desired world. The traveler remains in a state of limbo until their impersonator gives up their appearance.

Before I had time to read anything else, Morn and Bednik entered the room with Serrin and Bulrog. Everyone took a seat except Morn, who verbally reviewed our situation so far. When he had finished, he added, "Any suggestions as to our next course of action?"

"Set this up as our base instead of the ship?" I suggested.

"Good idea," said Morn. "More resources, more comfort, more room.

"It's also more secure and a better vantage point," added Kimara.

"Raid the town?" Bulrog piped up.

"Also a good idea," said Morn. "We may find supplies or clues as to our predicament."

"Or something bad might happen to complain about!" exclaimed Bulrog excitedly.

"Anything else?" Bednik asked us. Nobody had any more ideas.

"Tomorrow we move our supplies in here and scope out the town," said Morn.

Chapter 12
Unveiled Threats

It would be safe to say that I did not feel very safe upon waking up and finding the knife embedded in the floor next to my head. *Dark Magic* had been pierced through and was pinned to the floor with the knife. On top of the book was a parchment.

> Come to town. I'll be
> waiting.

I had slept on the carpet in the library that night, since I am not particularly fond of large, fluffy mattresses (and I was too tired to do much except crawl out of the chair). I quickly took stock of my surroundings. Kimara had fallen asleep reading in the chair next to mine. She had been the closest to me, so that made her the most likely suspect. Then again, whoever had done this would have done it and gotten out.

That raised another question. This was obviously a threat. Since whoever did this probably wanted us dead anyway, why hadn't they just killed me? Why hadn't they just killed us all and gotten it over with? Obviously someone was playing games with us. I tried to think of anyone I had met before in the crevice world who might fit that description, but nobody came to mind.

Then a sudden thought occurred to me: despite the fact that the storm had blown us drastically off course, our enemy had still managed to keep up with us. Somehow they were keeping tabs on us. This meant one of two things. Either it was someone in our group or the Dark Mirror had survived the storm. Perhaps whoever had put it there was still able to watch us even though I had hidden it under the barrels. They might have followed us here and found us in the house. We were dealing with someone very sinister and very smart.

Not knowing what else to do, I decided on the simplest course of action: eat. I found some snacks in the cupboards in the kitchen. I was munching on a roll when Serrin entered.

"Morning, Zeph," he said. "Sleep well?"

"Yeah, fine," I replied. "Except for the knife next to my head." He had turned his back to me and was rummaging through the cupboards, but when I said this he froze and slowly turned to face me.

"What did you say?"

"Last night, someone planted a knife clean through the book I was reading and into the floor. The book was right next to my head."

"Are you *serious?*"

"No, I'm joking," I said, calmly putting down my food. "Yes, I'm serious!"

"It's true, then," he said quietly.

"What's true?" I said. Serrin dropped his voice to a low, unsettling tone.

"Listen carefully, Zephyr, for this is a complex story and we haven't much time until the others wake up." He paused, as if trying to figure out where to begin. "Do you remember four years ago when you first came to the crevice world and I showed you the temple wall? Well, I wasn't entirely truthful. I told you that it said we had to go searching for humans each night in the next world. As it turns out, I actually knew

70

a bit more about what it said than I told anyone. What it really says is that the Oracle told Panok what to write on that wall. The Oracle is a..."

"I know what the Oracle is. Keep going."

"How do you know?"

"I'll tell you later. Just keep going."

"The Oracle told Panok that through the portal under the Galians' home was another world. In this other world was the key to saving us from Ranook. Panok wrote that in this world we would find a teenage boy who could rid us of this great evil. He never explained why it was you that had to destroy Ranook, only that it was you. Well, he was right. You did the job, and in spectacular fashion. But after you left, I went back to researching what he wrote. It turns out that Ranook was the first of three Dark Lords. He was destined to die at your hands. Whether the Oracle told Panok who the next two Dark Lords would be, I don't know, because if he knew, he never wrote it on the wall. What he did say was that the second Dark Lord could only be destroyed by you, just like the first one. But here's the catch: the final Dark Lord cannot come into power until you are dead. And you can't just die, you have to be killed by one of the remaining Dark Lords. This means that either the second Dark Lord is helping the third one into power, or the third one is helping himself. As far as what the rest of the wall says, well, I'm still working on it, but its condition isn't that great."

I sat there in a shocked silence.

"And you were planning on telling me this *when* exactly?"

"Well," he coughed uncomfortably. "I have been meaning to tell you for some time now."

"Oh, sure. The bad guy's objective is to kill me, and you're just *now* letting me know this."

"Well, it's just…all we have to do is kill him first."

"Oh, yeah! No problem! Since we're in familiar territory and we know exactly who the bad guy is and where his base is, we'll just organize our massive army and march right on up! What exactly are we going to do, bludgeon him with harsh language?"

"Don't get so hotheaded! All we have to do is analyze the situation."

"OK, you're right. Here's the situation: we have one weapon, six people, no clue what's going on, and no idea where we are. Oh, and someone just threatened my life."

"Someone who obviously knows where we are," said Serrin. "Which brings me to my next point: whoever did this is probably not one of the two remaining Dark Lords. Had they been, you would likely be dead right now. Obviously what they wanted to do was scare you."

"And get us to come to town."

"Pardon?"

"There was a note on top of the book. It said, '*Come to town. I'll be waiting.*'"

"Well, I guess we know what we're doing today."

"You don't actually mean to go out there, do you?"

"Unless you have a better idea."

"All right," I said after thinking a moment. "How about this: we gather our supplies from the ship like we planned, hole up in here, make a plan, figure out what the ding-hey we're doing, and then make a stealthy approach so we don't all get killed."

"I guess that works."

Struck by a sudden inspiration, I turned and made for the hallway. "Where are you going?" Serrin demanded.

"I have an idea. I trust you to fill the others in." Saying no more, I continued down the hallway. I had decided to survey the town more closely with the telescope upstairs and take notes on every little thing that could be used to our advantage. I made my way up the two flights of stairs until I reached the observatory.

I began searching for parchment and a quill to make notes. The most likely place for this seemed to be the trunks, so I tried those first. The first trunk I opened contained a book entitled *Tookie's Monster Scrapbook*. Under the book I found a variety of old cloths and cloaks. The next trunk contained what I was needed. It had a pile of unused parchment, a spare ink bottle, and some quills. Armed with these new tools, I made my way over to the telescope.

The town was, as Morn had observed, quite empty. The architecture resembled that of Tookie's house. The streets were made of cobblestone. I noticed the angular roofs and gables that could be used to make a hasty, somewhat risky escape if one had to be made. I was scanning the windows of one building when I noticed something else. People. That couldn't be right. The town had been empty when it was checked last. I adjusted the telescope. Sure enough, something with a human form was in the window of one of the buildings. It did not, however, seem fully human. As it turned out, there was another one lurking in the shadows. My first thought was that maybe they could help us. On closer inspection, I noticed that they seemed to be hiding. It was almost as if they were waiting in ambush for us. That wasn't a good sign. They had sort of a dark, crusty texture about them and I could not make out their faces.

Then a thought occurred to me. Maybe the scrapbook Tookie had made could tell me something about them. I picked the slim homemade book up from the trunk behind me and began flipping through its pages. There I found what I was looking for. A drawing of the creatures that waited for us in town sat next to the handwriting that read *Mudman*. My eyes scanned the entry.

> Mudmen are Dark Creatures made of, as the name implies, mud. They usually work in groups since they are not very bright. Despite their low intelligence, they are fierce and vicious fighters.

The description was kind of short, but the monster seemed simple. However, this complicated things a bit. There were probably many more of those monsters than I could see. Someone had set up an ambush. That meant that if we were going to get to the bottom of this, we would have to do so extremely carefully. We certainly couldn't stay here; someone already knew where we were and how to get in. And yet we couldn't venture out there, since we would probably get killed. This visit to the crevice world was turning out to be a lot less fun than I had planned.

And then I noticed something else through the telescope. Clouds. Gray clouds. They were far off in the distance, but they were coming toward us. *How can the clouds be gray,* I thought, *when the sky is amber?* When I saw the streaks below the clouds that meant snow, an idea began forming in my head. I returned to the trunk where I had found Tookie's

book. There I dug around in the cloth until I found
what I was looking for—some scraps of white cloth.
The plan would be risky, but it just might work.

Chapter 13
The Plan

After everyone had officially awakened and eaten, I updated them on our situation and informed them of my plan. We all agreed on our specific roles and set to work. Morn and Bednik took the canoe and began to load supplies from the ship (I made sure they got the mystery package Gorlub had given me). Bulrog and Kimara set about making small wooden platforms out of some wood from a scrap pile on the ship. Serrin and I went around the house making sure all the entrances were secure and gathering anything that could be used as a weapon. We had to work fast, as the storm was approaching slightly faster than I had anticipated. We took extra care to make sure that we could not be observed from the outside. Furniture was moved in barricades against windows. Blinds and curtains were drawn.

By the time midday arrived, we had finished our tasks. There was nothing left to do except stare out the cracks in our barricades at the storm. The snow probably would begin that night. We decided that we'd carry out the plan in the morning. In the meantime, we helped ourselves to a supply of slurk that had been brought from the ship. Or at least most of us did—Kimara sat in a corner and drank water, as she was not a big fan of slurk. We knew, although none of us voiced the thought, that if my plan went horribly awry, this would be the last time we ever sat and drank slurk like this. With this in mind, we spent the remainder of the day pretty much partying.

That night, we slept in shifts, with one of us up on sentry duty at all times.

It was early the next morning that the plan really began. We dressed warmly, putting on every scrap of clothing we could find. I took a moment to peer through one of the windows. It wasn't just snow. It was a blizzard. All the better for the plan, but all the worse for us. I was interrupted from my thoughts when Kimara spoke up.

"What happens if we get separated?"

"Try to get back here, and pray the Mudmen don't get find you," I said grimly.

Kimara buttoned up the pure white coat she'd found while the rest of us pulled on the makeshift cloaks we'd stitched together from the white cloth I'd found in the attic. We then retrieved the miniature wooden platforms that Kimara and Bulrog had built yesterday. They were just big enough to seat one person each, with a loop of rope up front to hold on to and steer with.

Once outside the house, I could barely see ten feet in front of me. We blended in very well, but I kept my sword ready just in case we needed extra invisibility or ran into something nasty.

We got a running start, then pounced onto our sleds stomach first. The six of us blended in perfectly as our sleds accelerated. The hill was a much sharper slope than it looked. Before long, we were zipping along at a brisk pace, weaving amongst each other dangerously. The peaks and gables of the approaching town suddenly became visible through the snow. Then we were in town, practically flying on the snow-covered streets. Here and there I caught a glimpse of the Mudmen, standing in windows or hiding behind corners. There had to be thousands of them. And then I caught a glimpse of the sleek black carriage standing in our path.

I yanked hard on the rope. I stopped, but I stopped by flipping over backwards into the snow. When I dug myself out, I saw that everyone else had stopped as well. The Mudmen still stood stock still. I stood up all the way and brushed off.

The carriage obviously had been meant to catch our attention, as something red had been splattered all over it. Morn sniffed it a few times, then shook his head. "It's just paint," he said. I inspected the writing on the side. *Legar and Lemario* was written in an arc of fancy gold calligraphy over the words, *Gypsy theatre, fortunetelling, ETC.* Someone had gone to a lot of trouble to put this in our path and make it eye-catching. "Let's go inside," suggested Bulrog.

The carriage was rather cramped inside, and had a lived-in look about it. There was a bed on the far wall and a cot rolled up in the corner. A window looked out on the town to our right. On the right of the window was a small bookshelf, but it was mostly loaded with bizarre items; skulls, crystal balls, and the like. To our left was a small pantry. And on the floor was the most eye-catching feature of all. I recognized it as the skull symbol servants of the Dark Oracle wore on their chests. It had been drawn in fresh charcoal, with a single word underneath: *Library.* "Is there a library in town?" asked Serrin.

"How should we know?" replied Bulrog.

"Well," said Bednik. "If there is, that's probably where we were intended to go next."

"So far, so good," added Morn. "I think we should be safe splitting up to look for it."

"Are you insane?" muttered Bulrog.

"We'll probably find it faster that way," pointed out Kimara. "Just don't do anything stupid."

"All right," I said. "Everybody go different ways and meet up in twenty minutes. There's a clock on the tower in the middle of town."

"This is crazy," Bulrog complained.

We filed out of the carriage and went in separate directions, dragging our sleds behind us.

Obviously, I do not know exactly what happened to the others, so I will only describe what happened to me. The first thing I did was draw my sword for extra invisibility. In the end I had to tie the rope on my sled to my belt because I couldn't drag it anymore. The snow had gotten too deep.

Every few feet I would see a Mudman hiding in a corner or alleyway. It was kind of eerie how they stood still, not breathing or even budging an inch. They just sat there. One could never tell what they were thinking or feeling, if they even thought or felt things. They had no expression. They didn't even have *features* to shape into expressions.

So far I had seen a blacksmith's shop, a cobbler's shop, a few homes, and several businesses, but still no sign of a library. I was about to turn around and head back when something caught my eye. It was a toy shop. Worn, faded colors and signage promoted the shop. I walked up to the frosty glass and peered inside. Dozens of rows of stuffed animals lined the walls. There was no sign of Mudmen inside, so I tried the door. It was open. I stepped inside and shut the door.

It was kind of warm inside. I wandered around for a few minutes inspecting the massive collection of stuffed animals, jack-in-the-boxes, puppets, and so forth. I went around behind the counter and leaned over it, staring out the window. Then I saw the music box. It was old and dusty and looked like it hadn't been used in ages. On the side was a name. It was a name that I never thought I would see anywhere again, much less here. *Ragnark*. It was impossible. It had to be a coincidence. It had to be somebody with the same name. There was no way it could be *our* Ragnark. It couldn't be the Ragnark that had died in battle with the evil Ranook.

I carefully lifted the lid. It was kind of a melancholy tune.

I looked again past the colorful toys into the snow as the creaky, mournful tune filled the room. I gave a small smile and left.

The snow had only gotten worse. One thing was different, though. The Mudmen were gone. Somehow, they had all just disappeared. This made me even more uneasy. They could be lurking anywhere. More importantly, what had caused them to move like that? I quickened my pace and tightened my grip on my sword.

I made it back to the carriage without incident and found Serrin waiting for me. "Any luck?" I asked. He just shook his head. I paused for a moment, unsure how to bring the subject up. Finally I just said, "What do we know about Ragnark's past?" He slowly looked up from the skull symbol on the floor.

"Why do you ask?"

"I found…something with his name on it." Serrin closed his eyes, sighed, and nodded slowly.

"He came to our village when he was very young," said Serrin. "I wasn't even born yet. We never knew about his past, we just accepted him. Well, you know he turned out to be Ranook's brother. I don't know where they came from exactly. Panok's journal mentioned something about it…it's a long story, but basically they came from a family of royalty. Well, I don't know if they'd exactly be classified as royalty. We don't have royalty in quite the same way it exists in your world. We don't have a *lot* of things as they exist in your world. I suppose the best way to describe it is, 'people with a lot of influence'. It's all in my notes somewhere. Anyway, the journal mentions that Ragnark ran away from home when his family became evil. That's all we really know."

"That's sort of vague."

"That's all we've got."

By this time, we saw a figure approaching in the snow. It was Bednik. He entered the carriage and shook his head to show he'd found nothing. "What happened to the Mudmen?" he asked.

"You noticed too, huh?" I replied. Serrin gave us a blank look. "All the Mudmen just slipped way when we weren't looking." I explained.

"That can't be good," frowned Serrin.

A few moments later, Kimara appeared, followed by Morn. "Good news," she grinned. "I found it." This was greeted by muted cheering, since we did not want to alert anything or anyone to our presence. The only thing we had to do was wait for Bulrog to return and we'd be off.

So that's what we did—we waited. And waited. And waited. And waited. And waited some more. You know what we did then? We waited. And waited. And…well, you get the idea. "Where *is* he?" Kimara asked.

As if in response to her question, a low, distant rumbling filled our ears. "What's that?" said Serrin, cocking his head quizzically. Then the form of Bulrog appeared, waving his arms and yelling something we could not hear. The ground began to tremble. Kimara's mouth dropped open as hundreds of thousands of Mudmen appeared behind him. Thinking quickly, Morn leapt to open the carriage door while Serrin pulled the wooden cover over the window and latched it. "BRACE FOR IMPACT!" I yelled. Bulrog bolted in the door, which was instantly slammed shut and locked behind him. The carriage jolted violently as the Mudmen slammed repeatedly into its sides. They banged on all four walls and rocked us back and forth.

"Well," said Serrin. "Things can't get much worse."

Chapter 14
Things Get Much Worse

It was as he said this that the carriage suddenly flew into the air, suspending all of its occupants. We floated in the air for a second before crashing back down. "THIS! IS! NOT! FUNNY!" I yelled. The carriage rolled over on its side again, causing us to tumble over one another and land in a heap on the ceiling as the objects from the shelves went flying around the tiny space.

The pounding on the walls became insanely loud. The wood was actually splintering. The floor (which was now above us) was cracking. It would break in a matter of seconds. I looked around, desperately trying to think of a plan. Then my eyes caught hold of the blanket that had fallen from the bed. If I could just grab it…my fingers curled around the edges and pulled it toward me. I pulled out my sword and tossed it to the ceiling (which was now below us) as I wrapped the blanket around me. "Grab the sword and don't let go!" I shouted as I rolled into a corner. I knew they wouldn't be able to lift it, since it was part of the sword's magic, but they didn't need to. I watched them shimmer and sort of slip out of focus as they grabbed the sword.

The floor splintered open with a tremendously loud *crack*. A couple of Mudmen dropped in. They were facing the other way, so I wrapped the blanket tighter around me and sneaked up behind them. They, of course, could not see the others and began looking around in confusion. I imitated their movements as best I could. So far they had not realized I wasn't one of them. I carefully reached up and hoisted myself out the hole they'd made in the floor. An army of them surrounded us. They all stood about milling around in confusion.

I jumped down into the crowd of Mudmen and began acting like one of them, pretending to wander around erratically. In reality, though, I was headed for the edge of the group. It was kind of rough going and the blanket almost fell off a couple times, but I made it. I was now standing on the outside of the group. I had to create some kind of diversion, but what?

Not knowing what else to do, I cast off the blanket and started yelling. "HEY! OVER HERE!" Some of the Mudmen in the back turned to face me. "YEAH! THAT'S RIGHT! OVER HERE! FREE FOOD!" About half the crowd turned to face me. "ALL YOU CAN EAT BUFFET! COME ON! THIS WAY!" The back of the crowd was starting to come toward me. By this time, even the front (though they were barely visible through the falling snow), had turned around. I started slowly retreating around the corner, making sure they were following me. They were. "FREE FOOD RIGHT THIS WAY! FREE FOOD! JUST FOLLOW ME!"

The whole lot of them was coming after me now. I suddenly wished that I had thought this out more than I had, but there hadn't been time. I kept retreating around the corner of a blacksmith's shop. I jumped in the door and locked it behind me, realizing it was only a matter of time before they smashed it open. I looked around me for anything and everything

I could use. Fighting was out of the question, since the others had my sword. I grabbed chairs, tables, shelves, tools, equipment, and whatever else I could find and piled them against the door. That would buy me a little more time.

The only way out was a creaky set of stairs that led to the second story. I took the stairs.

The second floor was rather sparse. A single bed was in the corner. A few windows provided some light. A ladder led to a trapdoor that I assumed led to the roof. I checked the situation outside from one of the windows. All the Mudmen had moved away from the carriage, which was jutting out at an odd angle in the snow.

There came a loud crashing sound from downstairs. They were about to break my barricade. I dragged the bed over to the stairs and pushed it down. Hopefully that would slow them down a little longer. There was a loud crash as the door ripped off its hinges and the furniture clattered inwards. That was my cue to make for the ladder.

I unlatched the trapdoor and slammed it shut behind me. I could not escape to the roof of another building. On the rear and left of this building lay two other buildings, but both had tall, peaked roofs that were inaccessible. Straight ahead, the ground was bathed in Mudmen. On the right, where the carriage was, there were only a few of them stuck in a traffic jam to get around the corner. That left only one way to go. I jumped off the roof.

The fall only lasted a couple seconds. The snow and my layers of clothing provided lots of padding. I checked to make sure the Mudmen hadn't noticed me, but they were still facing the other way. I sneaked over to the wagon and climbed inside. The others were waiting for me. "Brilliant, Zephyr!" said Serrin excitedly.

"Yes, good work," agreed Morn.

"Eh, you did okay, I guess," said Kimara reluctantly.

"We'll all die anyway," grumbled Bulrog.

"Well, *I* thought it was rather clever," said Bednik.

"Let's get out of here before they catch on," I said, sheathing my sword. "Kimara, lead us to the library."

The six of us climbed out the hole. I drew my sword again and everyone grabbed the hilt. We then sneaked carefully around the Mudmen, some of which had reached the roof and were now peering around in confusion. Once we were safely past them, I sheathed my sword and Kimara motioned us into a side alley.

"How is it," I said to Bulrog as we made our way through the dark alley, "that you managed to get *all* the Mudmen after you?"

"I burped," said Bulrog matter-of-factly.

"You *burped?*"

"Yup. I burped and one of the Mudmen noticed me and then they all came after me."

"Unbelievable. Our whole plan came unglued because of a burp."

We exited the alleyway and went onto another of the main roads. Then we took a left, went on for a bit, and stopped.

The library was easily forty feet tall, with a sharply angled roof. It was made of stone and had a massive door made of some kind of heavy wood. A few steps led up to the door. Morn and Bednik pushed on the door with a great deal of effort. A loud creaking split the howling wind.

Inside it was dead silent except for the creaking of the door and the loud grinding as Bednik locked it behind us. Light filtered in through the huge stained glass windows, catching specks of dust in midair. The bookshelves were so high it would take ladders to reach the top of them. A few hundred feet ahead was a small clearing with some tables and chairs. On either side of the clearing was a massive staircase that curved upwards until it reached a balcony with more bookshelves. Under the balcony were still more bookshelves.

The building was massive. We walked forward for a moment or two before reaching the clearing. On the table was a large parchment. On the parchment were some bizarre drawings and diagrams of what appeared to be a giant pair of wings.

"Hold on a minute," said Kimara. "These are blueprints. I can build these!"

"What are they blueprints *for?*" I asked.

"Some kind of...they look like wings or something."

"Wings? Why would we need wings?" inquired Bednik in a rather confused tone.

Just then we heard a strange noise off amongst the bookshelves. It was a sort of shuffling noise, combined with the sound of someone whistling. We frowned at one another, then peered around the corner into the bookshelves where the noise was coming from. A rather odd figure was coming out of the gloom down the bookshelves. It was tall, with long, spindly legs. It was pushing a cart full of books with one arm. The other three were shelving books. The other *three?* That couldn't be right. And yet there it was, plain for all to see. The figure clearly had four arms. It was wearing a suit that obviously had been tailor-made. The suit was a dark, grimy blue color with white pinstripes running the length of the thing. The figure itself was bald and had fair white skin similar to my own. This surprised me quite a bit, since I was not used to seeing people with skin any other color than green in the crevice world. The face was clean-shaven with sharp features and a hook nose.

"Welcome! May I help you find something?" it asked.

As you may have guessed, we were not really expecting to meet other people here, since the town and house had been deserted. We all had been caught completely off guard.

"Who are you?" Serrin finally said, breaking the awkward silence.

"I am the Head Librarian, or course." This caused us to look around awkwardly for another moment before Kimara spoke.

"We thought there was no one else here," she said.

"There isn't, really," the Head Librarian replied.

"But…" I started.

"Yes, I am here," he stated simply. "But sometimes I don't really play by the rules. Besides, when everyone else left, someone had to stay on to take care of the books."

"Where did they all go?" I asked.

"Well, they all just sort of disappeared. They didn't really go anywhere."

"So you know what happened, then?" said Morn.

"Of course. The Head Librarian sees all."

There was a slight pause as we waited for him to say more. When he remained silent, I said, "Well, what happened to everybody then?"

"I can't say," said the Head Librarian.

"I thought you saw all," I responded.

"Of course. I can sometimes even tell the future, which is why I can't tell you. I saw that in the future I would not tell you, which is why I can't tell you now."

"But you could just tell us and ignore that."

"I could, but then I would be wrong. I'm afraid you'll have to find out on your own. I will tell you, however, that the parchment on the table will help you find what you are looking for. I will also tell you that certain people here do not wish for me to tell all that I know."

"HA!" said Bulrog. "I bet you're lying! You probably have no idea what's going on! You can't see anything."

"I can indeed. Why else would I have an eye in the back of my head?" replied the Head Librarian, turning around to reveal that he did, in fact, have an eye in the back of his head.

"Oh yeah?" challenged Bulrog. "Well, if you're such a psychic, then try this one out. I'm thinking of a word, and it's not kitty."

"Kitty," said the Head Librarian instantly, turning smartly back around.

"GET OUT OF MY HEAD!" screamed Bulrog.

"And the reason I have so many arms is so I can multitask more efficiently, as all librarians need to do," he said to Serrin, whose jaw dropped. "And yes, your new invention will work," he said to Kimara, who let out an excited squeal and jumped about a foot in the air. "And yes, you look like a dork in that sweater." he said to me.

"Oh, well," I shrugged indifferently. "I don't really care."

Then came the sound of several fists banging on the door. "The Mudmen," said Kimara. We had to make yet another escape, and fast. She grabbed the parchment from the table and rolled it up quickly and carefully.

"Leaving so soon?" asked the Head Librarian. "What a shame."

"Yes, well, we'd love to stay for a bit longer," replied Serrin. "But there are other, more urgent matters that require our attention."

"Very well," said the Head Librarian. "So long!"

With that we departed up the staircase. We weren't exactly sure where we were going, but I think the idea was to hide. At least we could see what was going on from the balcony.

The door buckled and gave way with a tremendous *thud*. Hundreds of Mudmen poured in the opening.

"How is it," observed Kimara. "That they *always* know where to find us?"

"NOW, NOW!" shouted the Head Librarian from down below. "THIS IS A LIBRARY. PLEASE BE QUIET!" He was quite ignored by the Mudmen, who proceeded to knock over bookshelves and tables as they searched for us. "HEY! PLEASE RESPECT THE BOOKS!" They continued ignoring him. He was now getting quite furious. "THIS IS YOUR LAST WARNING!" When he could no longer stand to watch the Mudmen disrespect his precious books, he flew upon them in a fury, engaging them in fisticuffs. He was surprisingly strong and agile. Mudmen were sent flying left and right. Surprised at being attacked, they began setting themselves on him. However, the Head Librarian was much stronger than they had taken him for.

The whole crowd had moved into the building now, leaving the entrance open. The trouble was that the Mudmen were still blocking the staircase. My head started racing for a solution. Then I saw it: the bookshelves. I nudged Serrin and pointed at a long row of them. "You're kidding," he said.

"Why not?" said Kimara. "Looks like our only option." We looked at each other awkwardly for a moment, then I took the initiative. I leapt from the balcony and landed catlike on the bookshelf. I took off running while Kimara made the next leap. I used my momentum to leap over the Mudmen and onto the next shelf.

I reached the last shelf quickly in this fashion. There I tumbled off and landed on all fours on the stone floor. So far, so good. The Mudmen hadn't noticed me and the Head Librarian was holding his own easily. Kimara landed gracefully and silently beside me and the others were on their way. We slid out the door whilst the Mudmen still looked the other way. Once everyone was outside, we took off running.

Within a few moments we were back at the overturned carriage. We stopped in there to rest for a moment.

"The Mudmen aren't supposed to be that bright," I said once we were safely sheltered from the wind. "How do they keep finding us everywhere?"

"I don't know," grumbled Bulrog. "But I'm tired, hungry, cold, and wet, and we're all gonna die."

We spent a moment or two gathering our makeshift sleds we had left there before I crawled out the hole in the floor. As it turned out, stopping for too long had been a mistake. The Mudmen were rounding the corner of the blacksmith's shop.

We took off running (if you could call it that) through the deep snow, dragging the sleds behind us. The snow kept caving in underneath our feet, but we made it to the base of the hill okay. The progress up the hill itself was slow and tiring. The Mudmen were slowly gaining. My toes were numb from all the melted snow in my boots. At last the outline of the house became visible through the swirling snow. We slammed the door shut behind us and locked it. The house was already solidly protected against intruders, so we had some time to figure out our next move. Kimara unrolled the plans and laid them out on the floor. It was rather warm in here, so I took off my socks and boots and let them dry out.

"I think I can build these out of some of the stuff we have in here," she said.

"What are you standing around for, then?" snapped Bulrog.

Kimara instantly began scrambling around, gathering scraps of wood, canvas, and whatever else she could find. I double-checked our barricades on my numb, bare feet. So far they were holding up quite well. Morn and Bednik went upstairs to see what the situation was. Serrin helped Kimara start building. And Bulrog, not wanting to be left out, instantly and enthusiastically set to thinking about the most likely way we would all meet our ends and writing them out. A few moments later, Kimara stopped hammering.

"Are we going to need these sleds anymore?" she asked.

"Not likely," I said.

"Good, because I'm going to need the extra wood." She kept hammering for a moment, then paused with a funny look on her face. "Actually, we *will* need them."

"Why?" asked Serrin.

"Because I'm going to need more canvas," she replied. "And the only place to get that is from the ship's sails."

It was then that Morn and Bednik came down with some rather disturbing news. "We're surrounded," Morn announced. "There's no way out."

Chapter 15
Things Come Close to Getting Better, but Through an Ironic Twist of Events End up Getting Worse Still

"And there's something else," said Bednik. They sort of looked at each other awkwardly for a moment before he announced, "There's a castle floating in the sky."

"The second home!" Serrin blurted out.

"What?" I said, shooting him a funny look.

"When the Dark Oracle was created, three homes were built for it in case anything should happen. The second was a castle, rumored to float in the sky in the midst of a storm. I'd say it's safe to assume that the second Dark Lord is operating out of the second home of the Dark Oracle."

"Thus the reason for having us build the wings," realized Kimara. "So we can fly there."

"But we're stuck right now, as Kimara just said she needed the ship's sails to finish the wings, and we can't get to the ship if the house is surrounded."

"Most likely cause of death," stated Bulrog, writing on his list of probable ways we would all die. "Starvation from being cramped in house forever."

"Not necessarily," I said, getting an idea. "Do we have any gunpowder from the ship or anything?"

"I think so," replied Morn. "Why?"

Bulrog scratched out what he had just written. "Never mind that, then. New most likely cause of death: playing with fire." Ignoring him, I proceeded with my idea.

"Here's what we do. We're going to tie one sled in tow behind another. Then we drop the gunpowder with a lit fuse into the midst of the Mudmen on the porch. We blow them out of the way, then someone comes with me on the sleds to get the sail from the ship. We roll it up and tie it to the sled in tow, then come back up here."

Bulrog scratched out his writing and wrote something else. "Most likely cause of death: stupidity."

"No, no," I said. "It's only stupidity if we fail. If we succeed, then it's bravery."

"The Mudmen will follow you," said Kimara.

"We'll cut back through the woods and lose them," I replied. "Plus, we've got my sword. If all else fails, we'll just become invisible."

"Well," said Serrin, looking around. "I guess it's worth a try. I'm up to it."

"I'll go get the gunpowder," said Bednik, and left.

Once more, Bulrog scratched out an item on his list and wrote something else. "Most likely cause of death: being torn apart by large birds."

"Birds?" asked Kimara, shooting him a curious look. Bulrog shrugged.

"I was out of good ones, so I made one up."

"Okay, let's go." I said. "Kimara, it's up to you to tie those sleds together. Morn can help Bednik with the gunpowder. Serrin, let's get suited up."

Serrin and I began pulling our warmer clothes back on. I sneaked a peek out one of the windows. The Mudmen weren't there. I dashed up to the observatory as quickly as I could and found Morn, Bednik, and Bulrog waiting for me with a barrel of gunpowder.

"Hold on to that a minute," I said. I checked out front. No Mudmen. I checked out back. The Mudmen were there, but they were far off. In fact, they were moving *away* from the house. I wasn't sure what they were doing, but it couldn't be good. I double-checked the front of the house. There I caught notice of the castle. Sure enough, a large castle was floating in the sky, just as Morn and Bednik had described. The peaks and towers were impressively tall, seeming to stretch up into eternity.

Turning back to the three standing next to the barrel, I pointed out the fact that the Mudmen had all left.

"Hmmm," frowned Morn. "You're right. That's not a good sign. Look how methodical they're being. They're doing something. They're not abandoning us."

"Who cares?" said Bulrog. "Let's just take advantage of it. As long as they're not looking and we need the sails anyway, let's go."

Morn nodded slowly. "You're right," he said. "I don't like it, but we have to do it. Go ahead and get out there, but be quick about it."

I rushed downstairs and explained the situation to Serrin and Kimara. Kimara had already finished tying two of the sleds together, so we grabbed a third one for Serrin and set out instantly.

The air was still frigid and the snow still thick. Seeing no trace of the Mudmen, Serrin and I proceeded across the slippery, frozen porch. Once we were off it, we got on our sleds and pushed off. In a matter of seconds the wind was biting through my many layers of clothes. Navigating the path through the wheat was not a problem, since the snow had already buried it.

Even the streams had frozen over. This meant that once we reached the bottom of the hill, things got even hairier. The slick, frozen surfaces were difficult to navigate. All the while, we had to steer toward the ship, which wasn't easy to see in the snow. This was made all the more difficult by the fact that the snow was being driven directly into our eyes. Something else that made me uneasy was the constant presence of the Gochakra lurking underground. I didn't think it likely that they'd show themselves in this weather, but I was careful just in case.

Finally, we skidded to a halt in front of the ship. Serrin and I looked around to make sure everything was still. Besides the howling wind, there was no sound. I signaled to him to start climbing. The side of the ship was slippery and very dangerous. The railing was loaded with icicles. We carefully edged over it and onto the deck. It occurred to me that getting the sails off in this weather would be a nightmare. I was right.

The sail itself was partially frozen. This would complicate matters quite a bit. We had to climb out on the mast, Serrin at one end and myself at the other, to unfasten the sail. It fell to the deck and sort of just crumpled up. Serrin started down after it. I stayed up a moment longer to see if I could spot the Mudmen. There was no trace of them. Last I had seen, they were on their way to the woods, but now there was no sign of them. It was as if they had just vanished into thin air. Something was not right. They would not have just given up like that.

I proceeded down to the deck and helped Serrin roll up the sail. We were careful to be extra-quiet, just in case. I cut a rope from the ship's rigging with my sword and we tied the rolled-up sail onto the sled behind mine.

The ice was rather slippery, so we got a running start and pounced on the sleds. It would keep up for a while, then our speed would drop and we'd do it again. We reached the bottom of the hill fairly quickly this way. The going up the hill was toughest, since we had to drag the sleds and sail behind us. Before long, though, we found ourselves on the slippery porch and then inside.

Kimara had to drag the sail over to the fireplace upstairs to help the ice melt faster. In the meantime, she proceeded to disassemble the sleds. While the sail was drying out, she told us a bit more about the machine.

"It will have a wooden frame," she explained. "This will be topped with the canvas, which will catch the air. With the strong wind on our backs, this should carry about two people to the castle." We all looked around at each other, trying to decide who would be going.

"I want to go," said Bulrog, surprising us all. There was a brief pause as we considered it. "My brother lost his life in this quest. I'm going to finish what he started." He stared me defiantly in the face, a fierce look in his wide eyes.

"Well," sighed Morn. "I guess we can't deny him that."

"Who goes with him?" asked Serrin. There was a long pause. Then I spoke.

"I will."

"Fair enough," said Serrin grimly. Then they stared at me, mouths wide open.

"What?" I said. Then I felt something smash me into the wall. I crumpled to the ground. The pain was blinding, but I rolled over quickly enough to catch a glimpse of the Mudman stepping over me. Thinking quickly, Morn dispatched it with his sword and helped me to my feet.

Two more of them were coming down the hall. Shrugging off the dull ache, I drew my sword. Morn and I charged them, destroying them. "How did they get in?" I yelled in a frustrated tone.

"There must have been a break in the barricades somewhere," he said. "Split up and search the house. Kill any of them you find and fix however they got in!"

We almost bumped into each other splitting up, as I was invisible. He went upstairs and I rounded the hallway until I saw the others again. The door and window were properly barricaded. I checked the greenhouse, thinking that perhaps they had broken the glass and were getting in that way. I pushed through the shrubbery and vines until I reached the cherub statue. So far there was no sign of the Mudmen.

"ZEPHYR!" The shout made me hit the ground running. It was a female voice. Kimara.

I burst into the living room and found her backed into a corner by another Mudman. I sliced him clean in half. "HOW DO THEY KEEP GETTING IN?" I yelled. Serrin, Bednik, and Bulrog could do nothing to help, as they had no weapons. Another Mudman entered the hall. I beheaded it and charged down the hall. A Mudman stepped out of the bathroom. I stabbed him through, then turned back to the hall, trying to figure out where they could be coming from.

Another Mudman attacked from the bathroom; well, it couldn't see me, so it would be more accurate to say it bumped into me. In any case, I killed that one too. How had two Mudmen fit into the bathroom? My jaw hit the floor. *It couldn't be.* A third one was coming up out of the toilet. *The toilet. They were coming up through the sewer system.* "MORN!" I yelled. "BRING THE GUNPOWDER!" Then I sliced the one coming up. Sure enough, I could hear more of them coming up the sewer. I figured the pipe must have been built to funnel off into the woods. That must have been why they went to the woods. *How did they know where to look?* I thought as I neatly dispatched the next one.

Morn arrived with the gunpowder. "They're coming up the sewer!" I said. "We're gonna blast them out. Bring a burning log from the fireplace." He rushed off to obey as I killed another one. How did they know this place had a toilet? How did they know where the sewer pipe led? I hadn't even known these things.

I picked up the barrel and began pouring the acrid-smelling gunpowder into the toilet. Just as the barrel emptied, Morn arrived with a burning log. I grabbed it and dropped it into the toilet, then ran out of the bathroom.

From the hall I could see the toilet spewing flames as the muffled *boom* echoed throughout the house.

"That should take care of them for a bit," said Morn, wiping his brow. I sheathed my sword.

"We have to get out of here," I said. "It's only a matter of time before the next wave hits."

Back in the living room, Kimara, Serrin, Bednik, and Bulrog were working full swing on finishing the frame. "Ten minutes," said Kimara. "Give me ten minute and it'll be done."

"I don't know if we *have* ten minutes," I said in an exasperated tone. "How much longer do you think we have before they surface again?" I asked Morn.

"Hard to say," he said. "Five, seven minutes at most."

"Any more gunpowder?"

"One more barrel, I think."

"Get it. We'll need it." With that, I slumped over in a corner to try and get rid of the dull headache from being slammed into a wall. Morn ran off to fetch the last barrel of gunpowder.

I watched the others work on the frame for a moment or two. Then something occurred to me; Gorlub's package. He'd said it would help me whenever I was in real trouble. I didn't know what I'd encounter at the castle. I might as well take it with me.

I got up and slowly walked down the hall, rubbing the dull ache from my neck. The package was stored in the library. I picked it up and headed back down the hall.

When I got back, the others needed my help lifting the frame. Kimara said we had to move it outside to finish construction. There were no Mudmen outside, so I helped them lift it out the back door. The porch, though it was kind of slick, made a sort of hangar for the machine in progress.

"Zephyr," said Kimara. "Do us a favor and grab the sail from upstairs. We're almost ready for it."

On the way up, I encountered Morn, who was on his way down with a barrel of gunpowder. "Hurry up," he said in a strained voice. We don't have much time."

"Hang on, I'll be there in two seconds."

I hoisted the sail over my shoulder and hurried down the stairs as fast as I dared. I raced down the hall and around the corner of the library before yanking the back door open and throwing the sail to Kimara, who half-caught it with a bewildered expression on her face. I slammed the door shut and ran to the bathroom, where Morn had half-emptied the gunpowder into the toilet. "A log!" he yelled. "Get me a log!"

Once more I found myself bolting up the stairs as fast as my feet would allow. I was about to plunge my hand into the fireplace when it occurred to me that grabbing a burning log from a fire with your bare hands is not a very bright thing to do. Thinking quickly, I put on my glove and pulled out the top log. Then I rushed down the stairs again. When I got back, Morn had already emptied the barrel. I tossed the burning log down the toilet and we made a hasty retreat.

Another muffled *boom* echoed throughout the house. "Well, that's it," said Morn in a grim tone. "Let's hope she finishes those wings fast." That made a sudden, horrifying thought occur to me.

"What are you going to do to fight off the Mudmen when Bulrog and I leave?" I asked. He shrugged and smiled a small, sad smile.

"Whatever we can. Do try to hurry, though."

"We'll do what we can," I promised, choking back tears. Morn propped himself against the wall, his body falling limp.

By this time, Kimara and the others had finished the frame. I tied the package Gorlub had given me to the hang glider (that's pretty much what it was) and silently promised him to do my best. It was a matter of minutes before they finished attaching the canvas to the frame. Kimara stood back and surveyed her handiwork. "Well, there it is," she said proudly. Morn poked his head out the door from inside.

"More of them are on the way!" he shouted.

"Well, I guess that's our cue," said Bednik. "Good luck."

"See you two after the big guy goes down," said Serrin.

"And he will go down," muttered Bulrog.

Serrin and Bednik went inside to help Morn. "Now, remember," said Kimara. "Push off from the front of the house and angle up. And…and just in case I don't see you again…" she hugged us both and ran inside.

"Women!" said Bulrog indignantly.

We moved the glider around to the front of the house. It was indeed quite well built; it kept pulling up every time a gust of wind came along.

We were in front of the house now, facing the hill.

"Let's do this," I said, my face set in grim determination.

We pushed off.

Chapter 16
Revelations

A sudden gust of wind caught us under the wings and sent us flying up faster than expected. The ground rapidly fell away below us. We were airborne. The snow surrounded us. The castle loomed closer.

"I don't know if we'll make it!" I yelled over the wind. "I think we're too heavy!" Right as I spoke, two winged creatures flew overhead in a speedy blur. "What was THAT?"

"Uh…" said Bulrog. "Butterflies?" He was proven very wrong very quickly. The creatures looped back around and grabbed hold of our wings. It was then that I got a good look at their faces. They were gargoyles. Their skin had a stone-like texture to it. Their faces were wicked-looking. Their eyes were gleaming red. Long, sharp fangs dripped black, oily saliva. Their wings beat faster and faster, carrying our craft higher still. Bulrog and I hung on for dear life as we were buffeted by the winds.

The gargoyles carried us into a sort of hangar, then flew away. The hangar was made of some kind of mossy stone. Behind us was the open sky.

Straight ahead was a wooden platform. I took Gorlub's package off the hang glider and gripped it under my arm. Bulrog and I stepped onto the platform. Above us was the hollow inside of a massive stone tower. The platform lurched and began to move upward.

Every so often there would be a window cut in the tower so we could see just how high we were climbing. Eventually we could not see the ground at all.

Then the elevator stopped. Clutching the package tightly under my arm, I stepped forward into the pitch black room. A single lantern flickered to life, casting a small circle of pale yellow light on the wooden floor. A body was visible in the circle of light. It was facedown, but I could still recognize it. It was Gorlub.

Bulrog grimaced and looked away. A rasping voice echoed through the chamber.

"Welcome," the familiar voice hissed. "To the final challenge. Ssso far, you...have demonstrated...a talent for sssolving puzzlessss. I, the second Dark Lord, have one more...for you. In all the...challenges you have facccced, you have been...pressssented with the pieces to a larger puzzle. Now comes the time for you to...piece everything together. On the faccce...of thisss body...you will find what you need to ressssstore the world to its normal sssstate. All you have to do issss...look the body in the face."

Trembling, I knelt down and turned the body over. Gorlub's eyes were wide open. They stared at me, almost as if accusing me of something. His clothes were singed and burnt from the lightning.

Then something wet dropped onto the back of my head. I looked up. I was looking into a face I had seen before, but hoped never to see again. It was the Narissian King. The leader of the Nariss tribe that had double-crossed us and his own people in the war against Ranook.

"You!" I spat. "You're the second Dark Lord!"

"The one...and only," said the Narissian King, drawing himself up to his full, rather formidable height.

He was tall, with sleek, black skin and an oddly-shaped crest in the back of his head. A red slit on his forehead served as an eye. He had sharp fangs and wicked, curving claws. He was truly horrendous. "Congratulationsssss. I didn't think you'd have…the mettle…to look a dead body…in the face." A vicious look arose in Bulrog's eyes. He strode grimly toward the King.

"NO!" I shouted. "The prophecy says I have to do it, remember?"

His eyes still shone with fury, but he stepped back. The Narissian King was looking at him. This was my chance. In one smooth stroke I whipped out my sword and ran him through. I pulled out my sword. Thick purple blood oozed out the wound. The King looked down in mild surprise. Then the wound closed in an instant, disappearing entirely on its own.

"By the way," he hissed. "I have the power…of the Dark Oracle. The Dark Oracle controlsss reality."

"Only when it's backed with the proper power," I said, remembering the book I had read.

"Precisssssely. And right now, all the…people in…thisss world have been sucked into a…vortex. The dimension that the…Dark Oracle existsss on. It feedsss…from the power of their soulsss."

"There's a way to stop it," I said, holding him at sword point. "There has to be. How?" The King laughed.

"Oh, there'sss a way."

"How? Tell me!"

"What? Are you going to…kill me?" he said tauntingly.

He was right. Against him, Bulrog and I were essentially powerless. With the Dark Oracle controlling reality, we could do nothing. It was time to pull out all the punches. For every second that we spent up here, the others suffered at the hands of the Mudmen far below. We couldn't possibly search the whole castle. We were running out of time. I ripped the lid off the box Gorlub had given me. Digging through the layers inside, I pulled out the object that lay in the center.

I was thrown for a loop when I saw what it was. It was an object just small enough to fit in my hand without being seen from the other side. Its border was lined with skulls and its surface was a dull, soupy blue. I was staring at a Dark Mirror. The Narissian King uttered a low, dry chuckle that reverberated throughout the cold, dark room.

Bulrog shifted his eyes back and forth between us for a moment, then smiled a grim, dark smile. "Game's up," he said.

That was when Gorlub's corpse sat up. Shaking his head vigorously, he pulled himself to his feet. Through his tattered shirt I noticed what I had not seen before. On his chest was a skull. It was the same skull that Dark Masters branded their servants with. Gorlub had been branded.

"No way," I whispered.

"I'm afraid so," said Bulrog coolly. "Sorry you didn't notice sooner."

"So...so when you fell from the mast you were..."

"Branded, yes," finished Gorlub. "I've been waiting to receive mine for some time. After all, I've put in years of loyal service." My head was reeling. Gorlub and Bulrog were serving the Dark Oracle.

That was when it hit me. "You're not Gorlub and Bulrog!" I said. The puzzle pieces had just fallen into place. "Whoever is underground is immune to the Dark Oracle's vortex. Gorlub and Bulrog weren't with us in the village of Yoen! When everyone was transferred to the Dark Oracle's plane, they were in transition between two worlds. You hit them with a placeholding spell! That's how you knew you were going to leave soon. You were about to get branded. You guys used the Dark Mirrors to spy on us and report back to him!"

"Very astute," sneered Bulrog's impostor. "Give him up," he said to Gorlub's impostor. The two began to morph before my eyes.

The one that had been Gorlub was wearing a long, black cloak with the hood down. His eyes were a fierce yellow. An unruly mop of blue hair adorned his head. He was rather young, perhaps sixteen or seventeen. He had a large nose and bushy eyebrows that shaped themselves into a perpetual scowl.

The one that had been Bulrog was a bit taller. He also wore a black cloak, but the hood was pulled up and the head lowered.

"Legar," he said coldly.

"And Lemario," said the other.

"Father," said Legar.

"And son," said Lemario.

"Gypsy theatre, fortunetelling, and more," finished Legar.

"That was your carriage we went into," I realized aloud.

"We rather pride ourselves on the acting part," said Lemario. "I think those roles were rather expertly played, if I say so myself."

"Well, that explains…a lot." I said, at a loss for anything else to say.

"Enough!" roared the King. "We are…wasting time. Let usss kill him now."

"No!" said Legar. "Remember, we read the prophecy first, then we do it."

"Why?" said the King. "Forget...the prophecy! Kill him firsssst!"

Ten or twelve Mudmen stepped out of the shadows with the chunks and pieces of the temple wall and dumped them on the floor. Legar knelt over it and waved his hand mysteriously. The pieces of the wall flew together and mended perfectly. Once again the wall was whole. The hieroglyphic-like writing was once again complete.

All except for one piece. The piece around my neck. Their primary attention was on the wall, so I quietly tucked the necklace under my shirt where it could not be seen. Legar scanned the wall quickly, then noticed the missing piece. "WHERE IS IT?" he roared, turning to face me. Well, in retrospect, he didn't really face me. He was careful that the hood cast a shadow over his face.

"Where is what?" I said innocently.

"Don't play games with me," he said, stepping closer.

"Someone's been playing games with me this whole time," I replied.

The backside of his hand struck me across the face. "Give it to me or else."

"Or else what?"

"Or else you die."

"Does the prophecy say I die today?"

I had caught him. He hesitated for a moment. And in that moment, the Narissian King acted. Without warning, his claw ripped through my chest, ending my life in a matter of a second.

Or at least that's what would have happened if Lemario hadn't been so quick on the uptake. He produced the sword out of nowhere, neatly slicing off the King's claw. The Narissian King screamed in pain. "Do as my father says," declared Lemario through clenched teeth. "And my father says to do as the prophecy says."

"The prophecy says," announced Legar. "That Shu'ra, king of the Tur'qa Nariss tribe and Second Dark Lord, must die at Zephyr's hands. His protection by the Dark Oracle has been revoked."

"NO!" the King yelled. He was too late. I had drawn my sword and run him through. The wound did not heal this time.

In his dying throes, the King tried to lash out at me, but as he could not see me, struck Lemario instead. Lemario gasped. The tail of the King had just run him straight through. He turned his head pleadingly to his father. "Dad…"

"No matter how much it grieves me," he said, his voice trembling with emotion. "The prophecy must be obeyed."

His son stared at him, begging him with his eyes to help as his life spilled out onto the ground in the form of his blood. "I can't," said Legar quietly. And with that, his son died.

"Now," he said, trying to control his emotion. "I know the whole story but the end. Give me the end."

"No," I said firmly. A vicious right hook landed across my jaw and sent me to the floor. It was followed with a harsh kick to the stomach.

"Are you going to give it to me, or will I have to resort to…harsher measures?"

"Bring it," I said, pulling myself up and grabbing my sword. "You're not going to kill me today. You can't."

His hand grabbed my sword. Somehow, Legar could see me. His blood ran down the blade. He didn't flinch; indeed, he did quite the opposite. He impaled himself on the blade, walking slowly towards me until it protruded from his back.

That was when I caught a glimpse of his face. All I could see this close was an eye. It was an eye set with fierce determination, weathered with many years of sorrow and pain. Underneath the eye was a design etched in black makeup. It was a sort of spike that extended down to his cheek.

"Well," he said with a hint of sadness. "There's nothing I can do here. Enough have died here today," His voice turned hard as stone. "We lose for now, but we will gain the prophecy later. This is not over. We will meet again!" He turned and strode off into the darkness, shadows obscuring his face once more. As he left, I saw his wounds close up like the King's had.

The second he was out of sight, the Mudmen disintegrated into thin air. The Mudmen weren't the only thing. The whole structure began to crumble. Then the floor gave way beneath me, spilling me out into open air. I blacked out.

Chapter 17
Tomorrow

I wasn't entirely sure where I was when I awoke. It was hard to tell if I was alive or dead. All I could see was white. I tried sitting up.

I was on the sofa in Tookie's house. The sounds of something festive could be heard coming from outside. "Oh, good, you're up," said Kimara. She was sitting on the edge of the table, leaning back.

"What happened?" I asked.

"The dragons did," she replied. "Whatever you did up there, you must have done something right, because all these people just came spilling out of nowhere. There was a local band of dragons, too. They saw the castle collapse and you fall, so they broke your fall. You might have drowned if they hadn't. The castle moved out over the ocean."

"The ocean?" I repeated, a cold fear gripping me. "It's lost, then…"

"What's lost?"

"Panok's prophecy…the temple wall…it's gone. We could have known how all of this turn out…they had it in the castle. It must have fallen to sea." I checked my necklace to see if it was still there. It was. "This is the final piece of the prophecy. This is how everything ends." I started to take it off. She put her hand on mine, holding it in place.

"Maybe some things aren't meant to be known," she said softly.

"This may not reveal anything anyway," I said. "The rest of the prophecy didn't mean much without this piece, maybe this piece doesn't mean much without it."

"What happened up there, anyway?"

"It's a long story. Wait until we're with the others and I'll explain everything. What happened down here?"

"Morn managed to hold off the Mudmen for a bit. Then Bednik remembered you saying something about the Gochakra—something about how they ate dirt. We ran down the hill and woke them up on purpose, then led them here. They took care of the Mudmen for us. Then the snow stopped and all the Mudmen just disintegrated. That's when everybody just appeared." She allowed a pause before fearfully inquiring, "What happened to Bulrog?"

"That wasn't Bulrog."

"Huh?" she shot me a blank look.

"That wasn't Bulrog. He was an impostor, a fake. The same goes for Gorlub. They...it's complicated. Wait until everyone else is here so I don't repeat myself."

"Actually, you'll have to go out there. Everyone else is busy partying."

"All right," I said, and got up. I followed her out front, where a party was indeed going full swing. Children chased after each other in lively games of tag. Blankets had been spread out on the ground and were being used as makeshift buffet tables. I grabbed a roll and smeared it with dragon's butter before catching up with Serrin. He was chatting animatedly with Morn and Bednik, in the midst of exaggerating a tale about how he had single-handedly fought off an entire gang of Mudmen using only a fire poker.

"Sorry to interrupt," I grinned. "But I've got something to brag about myself."

"Hey, Zeph's up!" said Bednik.

"What happened to Bulrog?" Morn asked instantly. I took a bite of my roll and stared up at the amber sky before beginning the tale of what happened in the castle.

When I had finished, there was a long pause as everyone digested the facts I had just revealed.

"I guess," said Serrin. "That when we get back, the others will be waiting for us."

"Oh, that reminds me," said Morn. "I talked to a couple of local workers and they've agreed to help us repair the ship. We should be on our way by tomorrow."

"That's good," I replied without much emotion. "When we get back, I'd better...go..." Nobody said anything. I just started walking down the hill, hands in pockets. I didn't know where I was going, and I didn't care.

Within a couple of minutes I was walking down the main road in town. There I saw the overturned carriage. I paused to look at it. I was the only one. For some reason, the party was in full gear on the hill, but there was almost nobody down here.

Who was Legar? Who had Lemario been? How did they fit into all this?

Somehow, at that exact moment, I didn't care. I just kept walking, turning at random through the maze of snow-covered cobblestone streets.

I didn't realize where I was going until I got there. A large window stood in front of me. Behind the window were colorful rows of stuffed animals, jack-in-the-boxes, puppets, and other such toys. I was in front of the toy shop again. I wondered where the

116

owner was. Maybe they were on the hill with everyone else. Somehow I had a feeling that wasn't the case.

"It's deserted, you know," said the voice from behind me. It was a small, sad-looking man. "Didn't expect to see any humans here." He had an unruly mop of dark hair that looked like it had never seen a comb. A pair of piercing green eyes sat in the midst of a hollow, gaunt face.

"I came from…somewhere else. I was helping against the Dark Oracle."

"Why aren't you at the celebration, then?"

"I could ask the same of you," I replied. He smiled a sort of sad smile.

"I'm never at celebrations. I don't have much to celebrate."

"What's your name?"

"Tookie."

"No way! We were working out of your house!" I blurted, before realizing how weird that sounded. "Sorry…"

"Oh…" he said. "I knew I should have cleaned it up a bit more."

"Don't worry about it," I said, relaxing considerably. "Go on ahead and join the party."

"No, no," he replied. "I'll just sit here. You go ahead."

"I insist."

"Well," he said, taking a deep breath. "I'll go if you go."

"Fair enough," I laughed.

With that we set on our way back up the hill. "You must be the one mentioned in the prophecy," he stated cautiously.

"How did you know about that?"

"I've spent most of my life researching the bizarre and unusual, you know."

I paused a moment.

"Yeah, I'm the one," I said.

"That's really interesting," he replied in an awed tone. "You should write a book."

"Maybe I will," I grinned.

Once we were up the hill, I introduced Tookie to Serrin and the others, then left them. I went around to the back of the house, where I could see the Gochakra wandering about. Beyond the Gochakra were the sails of the ship. A small team of men was working on it.

I would have liked nothing more than to stay in the crevice world longer. However, it would be morning soon in my world and I needed to get back.

"Morn says it'll be done and ready to go tomorrow," said Kimara. I hadn't noticed her sitting behind me.

I took another look at the necklace. She was right. Maybe some things weren't meant to be known.

I lay down in the snow and stared up at the sky. Tomorrow was soon enough.

Disclaimer

At the end of most books, you will find a disclaimer telling you that the events of that book are a work of fiction and the characters are merely figments of the imagination. This is not quite the case with this book.

The references to real people are entirely intentional. As unlikely as it may seem, all the events in this book are not works of fiction. But then again, not everything is what it seems.

In my last book, there was a picture of me standing next to the green conversion van that has the link to the crevice world. This time, however, I have brought something much more fascinating. Proof of the crevice world itself. Sometimes it hangs around my neck on a black shoestring (the original string broke). It is the ending of the story. It also exists as a symbol. A symbol that proves that other places do exist, and that we can get there.

All it takes is a little imagination.

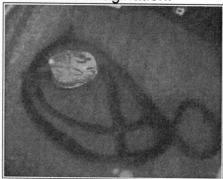